PRINCES IN WAITING

PRINCES
IN
WAITING

L ARRY G ASPER

COTEAU BOOKS
WWW.COTEAUBOOKS.COM

© Larry Gasper, 2004.

Edited by Edna Alford.
Book and cover design by Duncan Campbell.
Cover image, "Two Men Arm Wrestling," © Patricia McDonough/Photonica.

Printed and bound in Canada at Gauvin Press.

National Library of Canada Cataloguing in Publication Data

Gasper, Larry, 1951-
Princes in waiting / Larry Gasper.

Short stories.
ISBN 1-55050-291-3

I. Title.

PS8613.A86P74 2004   C813'.6   C2004-901623-7

1   2   3   4   5   6   7   8   9   10

COTEAU BOOKS
401-2206 Dewdney Ave.
Regina, Saskatchewan
Canada   S4R 1H3

Available in the US and Canada from:
Fitzhenry & Whiteside
195 Allstate Parkway
Markham, Ontario
Canada   L3R 4T8

The publisher gratefully acknowledges the financial assistance of the Saskatchewan Arts Board, the Canada Council for the Arts, the Government of Canada through the Book Publishing Industry Development Program (BPIDP), and the City of Regina Arts Commission, for its publishing program.

The Canada Council for the Arts
Le Conseil des Arts du Canada

SASKATCHEWAN ARTS BOARD

Canada

Regina
CITY OF REGINA

To my mother,
for all those nights reading
*to my brothers and m*e

CONTENTS

OLD MEN
WEARING HATS

I slowed the car down as we pulled up behind a shiny new Cadillac, and snuck a glance at Mac. Eyes narrowed against the bright sunlight, he looked straight ahead at something I couldn't see, something he didn't want anyone to see. I tapped the brakes as we came up on the Caddy's back bumper. All I could see in the driver's seat was a straw hat with grey hair sticking out from under it. Typical.

"C'mon, you old fart, move it." I swerved the Mustang out, then back in quickly. Way too many cars and campers heading out of town to the lake for the Victoria Day long weekend. I settled in to wait for a break in traffic and tapped my fingers on the console. "Jesus, Mac, look at that. A goddamn Caddy and he can't get over forty."

MacAllister mumbled something.

"What?" This was the first thing he'd said to me since he asked for a ride to Prince Albert.

"I said there's no hurry."

I took a quick look at him and frowned. "You're the one that was in a panic to get to town today. Christ, we're wasting a day off and now there's no problem following some old dwarf that has to stare through the steering wheel? What's with you?"

"Nothing! Just pass the old guy if you're in such a big shitting hurry."

"Okay." I took a quick look, shifted down and punched it. The thrum of the V8 changed to a roar as we jumped into the other lane and rocketed past the old man. I swerved back into our lane in front of him as a pulp truck went by, horn blaring.

"Yeah, yeah, tell it to that old fart back there. It's all the old men wearing hats driving their land boats that are the problem, right Mac? Mac?"

"Just drive." Mac reached over and turned the stereo back up and The Cars blasted out of the speakers. I shrugged and settled in at eighty, the trees whipping by, traffic light heading into Prince Albert with the holiday and everything. Mac had sunk back into his funk and damned if I could figure out what to do with him. You'd think that after almost twenty years as neighbours and friends I could get through to him, but he didn't talk about himself any easier now than when we'd been kids. Oh, he'd talk all right, he was a MacAllister after all, and any one of them could talk your ear off, but it was all stories and jokes. Good stories and jokes, but only stories and jokes all the same. His brother Brad wasn't like that but I hadn't seen him in the two years since he'd moved out. Darchuk saw him once in a while in

Saskatoon. Getting ready to go to university, yet. Christ, we'd thought it was a big deal when Mac almost made it all the way through high school, but Brad had always been different. A reader, a thinker, a dreamer. Tough thing to be for a MacAllister, especially with Old Red for a grandpa.

Old Red. Now that could be what was riding Mac, but I couldn't see why. Red was tough, a narrow-minded old tyrant who'd always figured that he needed to beat Mac and Brad to keep them in line when Mac's dad was away on one of his runs, which was most of the time. Bill was never one for sitting still when he could be in a semi, driving to God knows where, just as long as it wasn't Pine Valley. Not that he was any prize, but Bill was fucking Ghandi next to Red. He had only used a belt on the boys, while Red used a chunk of harness leather. Even though he kept it well oiled, it was still more like a club than a strap. Bill had a lot fewer rules than Red. And you could tell which way Bill was going to jump when he was drunk. Not like Red. Or Mac lately.

Of course, with all the problems in his family the last little while it was natural he was fucked up. His grandma dies, his grandfather ends up in a home, his mom leaves his dad and moves to Saskatoon, and his dad blames him for it because he thought Mac had given her money and told her to leave. With the two of them living in the same yard, Mac in his grandparents' house and Bill in the family house, it made for a strange situation. Only in the MacAllister family, as Radinski had said. Definitely time for that good drunk tonight to take

Mac's mind off things. We were looking at a whole month up on the Churchill rail line starting Tuesday, so this trip to town was cutting into valuable drinking time.

"Hey, Mac," I yelled over the stereo, "we got anything else to do besides pick up that new starter for your truck?"

"Maybe."

"Maybe what?" I said, turning the volume down. "You need grub or can we hit the bar for a couple?"

"No, I don't need grub." Mac rubbed his face. "Look, I've got something to do, someone to see. How's about you have a beer while I do that. It shouldn't take long."

"You've got to be kidding. You know nobody else drives the 'Stang."

"I ain't going to wreck your precious Mustang. I've just got something to do. Something personal." The last two words came out harsh, angry. I slowed as we approached the bridge interchange and tried to figure out what the hell was going on. The car wasn't that big a deal. It wasn't like Mac was half in the bag or anything and he'd get to play with my new toy sooner or later. But not until I figured what was what.

"You got a woman in town or something?" I grinned at him. "If you do, she better have her own place, cause the back seat in this thing is a bitch to fuck in."

"It's not a woman." Flat, emotionless. Where the hell had his sense of humour gone?

"Okay, Mac, if you want to act like you've got a stick shoved up your ass, fine by me, just make sure I'm not around for your next fight. I'm tired of cleaning up after you, making excuses for you."

"Nobody asked you to."

"Nobody... You know Mac, you can be a real prick sometimes." I stopped the car at the lights at the end of the bridge. Asshole. Sometimes I wondered why I tried so hard. So he'd had a rotten childhood. Tough shit. Time to get over it. For now he could just stew in his own juices. Maybe that would get him thinking about things enough that he might talk when he'd had a couple of beer.

We drove through Prince Albert slowly, traffic heavy on Second Avenue, the lights against us most of the time. I itched to use the Mustang's power, but had to putt along until we were up on the hill, past the mall. Traffic lightened up and I opened it up a bit. I smiled as we drove by the Ford dealership and I saw a new black Mustang on display outside. Another '82 GT. I started to say something to Mac about there being a matching car for him, but stopped in time. Even though we'd made good money away from the farm the last couple of years, Mac didn't have a pot to piss in and, though he never said a word, we all knew it was because he was saving for his brother Brad's university. Not that Mac would ever tell us that. MacAllister family business. They were weird that way. So between the railroad this year, and the bush last winter, I had the Mustang, Radinski had his Trans-Am, and Hicks, pussywhipped as he was, and having lots of daddy's money, had spent his money on an engagement ring. Mac, though, he still drove his old beater half-ton that'd had the bag driven off it. He spent more time under the hood of that thing than he did driving it.

We cleared the edge of the city and turned onto the gravel road out to the junkyard. I tapped my finger in time to The Cars singing "Candy-O" as we pulled up in front of the shack that passed for the yard's office.

"Mac, we can go back to Ford and get a new starter if you want. I'll lend you the money."

His forehead creased, then he smiled, sharp and humourless. "No thanks. It'd kill that old piece of shit of mine if it ever got a new part put in it."

I chuckled. Not the old Mac, but a start. He climbed out of the car, then picked up his tool box from the back floor.

"Need any help?" I asked.

"Nah. Only take me a few minutes. Relax, listen to some tunes. Let your beard grow or something."

I winced. We'd started a beard-growing contest when we got on with the railroad and I'd hoped for less baby-faced or more distinctive. Instead, I'd ended up with a moustache not even a fourteen-year-old could love and a blond scruff under my chin that was several shades lighter than my hair. Mac's beard, on the other hand, had come in almost as a goatee, sharpening his face to a knife edge. If it wasn't for his freckles, there wouldn't have been a hint of softness on his face.

Mac started to turn, then stopped and stood still for several seconds. With his back to me, he said softly, "I want to go see Gramps," then he strode past the office and into the rows of wrecked cars sitting on blocks, hoods missing, engines, windshields, doors gone. In seconds he disappeared into the fourth row.

6

"Shit." I rolled the window down all the way, leaned over to do the same on the passenger side, then popped the tape out. So it was Old Red. No wonder Mac was all twisted. Victoria Day weekend two years ago was the last time he and Red had tangled, the last time he'd had much of anything to do with Red until Red's accident, just before they'd put the bastard in the old folks' home. I put the cassette in its case and dropped it into the console, picked up Pat Benatar. I felt a hard grin, a Mac grin, flit across my face. Pat's "Hit Me With Your Best Shot" sure as hell fit right now. I popped it in and leaned back in the seat, eyes closed against the sun.

That day had been a lot like today, warm for May, muggy, with a good gully washer only a day or two away to ruin all the campers' fun. It was Saturday and Mac and I had been picking rocks on the Johnson quarter. We'd finished up early and I'd pulled Dad's half-ton into Mac's yard around four in the afternoon, right into a whole pile of shit.

Mac's sixteen-year-old brother, Brad, lay on the ground trying to squirm away from Red. Red's arm was raised above his head, the strap a dark line against the sky. Mac bailed out before I even stopped, his fist smashing into Red's face as he turned. Red went over backwards, dust puffing up as he hit the hard-packed dirt. Brad scrambled away, tears running down his face. I jumped out of the truck and ran over to him as Mac hovered over his grandfather.

"Stay down, old man. You don't want to get hurt," Mac rasped, but I heard an edge of fear. This day had been a long time coming, but eighteen years of terror aren't erased by winning a couple of fights. Of course, there was never a MacAllister with the brains to take the smart way out, so the old man had gotten up.

"Whipped your ass when you tried this two years ago, boy, and I'll do it again." Red lifted his fists and smiled at Mac, his eyes bright with the MacAllister wildness. "Take your best shot, you little fucker."

Mac smiled, his eyes just as wild, his feet set, hands fisted tight. "You don't know how long I've waited to do this, Gramps. I'm not a little kid you can beat on anymore."

"I whipped bigger than you before. Your dad never could do it and you sure the hell can't."

"I ain't the old man." Mac bobbed in toward Red, ducking Red's wild punch easily. I stood by Brad, unsure what to do, whether to try to stop it or get Mac's mom. He might listen to her, though I wouldn't have bet on it. His dad he'd just swing at. Good thing Bill was away on a run. As usual. I took a step toward the house, then stopped as Brad grabbed my hand.

"Don't. Andy can do it."

I looked down at him. His glasses sat crookedly on his face, his left eye already swelling, his face red where his grandfather had smacked him. He clenched a notebook. I gently tugged it from his hands and looked inside. Poetry. Yeah, that'd be enough. I handed it back to him.

"It's not Andy I'm worried about," I said, looking at the two tall men circling each other, fists flicking out to take the other's measure, their boots kicking up dust.

"Why would you worry about that old bastard?" he said. It was the first time I'd heard him swear.

Good question. I remembered Mac screaming as Red's strap whistled through the air before cracking across his ass and legs. And I remembered the pain slicing through my legs the one time Red caught me, the blue and green of the bruises, the agony of trying to sit, to walk. And I thought of how Mac and Brad had lived through that year after year, not just once.

"Yeah, why would I?" I knelt next to Brad and bit my lip.

Red circled Mac, smiling as Mac flinched when he feinted. My stomach knotted. Red was over forty years older than Mac and there was grey in his hair, but he was still a vicious old scrapper, as tall as Mac and thicker through the body. Then I remembered Mac at the dance in Spruce Home last weekend. The guy outweighed Mac by forty pounds but Mac turned his face into hamburger in under a minute. Radinski and I had barely got Mac off him. And Mac had still been ready for the guy's friends.

Red's left shot out and Mac caught it on the cheek as he tried to slip it. A right and a left followed but Mac blocked them easily. He shook his head, touched his cheek and the fear faded from his face. His left flashed out and cracked against Red's nose. Blood gushed out. Mac danced to his right, breathing easily, his left darting through Red's guard again and again, rocking Red's head back, knocking his hat off, splitting his lip, putting a welt under his eye. The wildness was still in Mac's eyes, but it was cold, cold and calculating, not the heated, berserk rage of his other fights, and the coldness ran through me, leaving the heavy weight of fear in my belly.

Red gulped for air as he swung a haymaker that Mac easily sidestepped. Mac stepped into Red and drove an uppercut into his stomach. Red's eyes widened, the wildness leaving them as his hands dropped to his sides. Mac grabbed the old man by the shoulder and slugged him in the stomach two more times, then pushed him away.

"C'mon, old man, you can do better than that. That wasn't even my best shot. Or maybe you need your fucking strap to beat me?" Mac drifted backwards, leaving Red bent over and wheezing in the middle of the yard, eyes blank – old – over the blood-smeared mess of the rest of his face. His laboured breathing was the only sound I could hear as Mac knelt and picked up the strap. I looked at the house, hoping to see Mac's mom coming out the door. He was too far gone to stop for anyone else and I couldn't pull him off Red by myself. But as I watched, the curtain closed in the kitchen window and despite the heat I shivered. Mac's mom was as scared of Red as we were, but to let your son do this to his own grandfather?

"Andy's not the only one that got hurt trying to protect me," Brad said as he followed my gaze. I nodded and swallowed, my mouth dry. I'd never known just how bad things were at Mac's. Never wanted to know actually. I understood why he tried to spend as much time as he could at our place or Radinski's, but I never let myself see just how bad the situation was.

Mac came back at Red, slapping the strap across his hand, the thick leather clapping loudly. He smiled, his eyes ice. "You always liked this thing, didn't you, old man," Mac said, waving the strap in Red's face.

Red slapped it aside. "I'll shove it up your ass, you little punk," he rasped, but the old power wasn't behind the words and I even thought I heard that edge of fear I'd heard in Mac's voice earlier.

Mac laughed. "Anytime," he said and flicked the leather across Red's face. Red stumbled back, his hand going to the welt on his cheek. I saw the wildness come back into his eyes and started to shout to warn Mac, but Red let out a yell and charged before I could even open my mouth. Mac had the strap raised for another blow when Red slammed into him. It was Mac's turn to stumble backwards, then fall as Red kicked the feet out from under him. The strap fell from his hand.

Red jumped on Mac, right fist pistoning into his face. Brad started to get up and I pulled him back down. This was the type of fight Mac loved, down and dirty, no skill, just root hog or die.

"Easy now," I said as Red pulled his fist back. Mac arched his back and Red slid half off him. Mac grabbed a handful of Red's hair and yanked as he twisted out from under the old man, then he rolled fully clear, jerked Red's head down and threw a punch across his body, then another. His fists smacked into Red's face as he twisted the old man's head till his body was sideways. One of Red's hands scratched at the hand locked in his hair, while the other waved in front of him in a futile attempt to stop the punches. Mac pulled his legs up, then rolled to his knees. His fist pounded into Red's face, once, twice, three times, the blows echoing across the yard. I started to stand, to grab him before he killed the old man, but finally Mac stopped and pushed Red's face into the dirt.

Red made a thin, keening whine as he struggled to get to his hands and knees. Mac pushed him down with his boot.

"Stay down, you old fucker. I ain't sixteen this time and I can do this anytime you try me." Mac walked over to where the strap lay in the dirt. He picked it up and tossed it to Brad. "Show him how it feels."

"Mac, no – " I said.

"Shut up, Ken." He looked at his little brother. "Do it."

Brad held the strap in both hands, shaking, whether from fear or excitement I couldn't tell. For the first and only time, I saw the MacAllister wildness in his eyes. I shoved my hands into my pockets to hide my own shaking as Brad stumbled over to Red, the strap held like a baseball bat in his hands. He jerked to a stop by the old man, raised the strap high over his head like an ax, then brought it slashing down across Red's ass.

Red screamed. He tried to roll away and the next blow nailed him in the nuts. He screamed again and drew himself into a ball. Brad sobbed as he brought the strap down again and again, looking for all the world like he was chopping wood. He was screaming at Red as he swung, the chant of "Bastard, bastard, bastard" keeping time with the smacking strap.

"This is crazy, Mac," I said, stepping toward Brad. Mac grabbed my arm, fingers digging into my bicep. I jerked free and stepped back. "Christ, you won. You don't want Brad to end up in jail."

He stood, tall and rigid, ice-green eyes fixed on Red, face set. "I won't let him kill the old fuck, but he brought it on himself."

"Jesus, Mac, listen to yourself. This is way past pay-back."

He swung his head to look at me. "Is it?"

I met his gaze and swallowed. I didn't know this Mac, this Mac who had grown in pain and silence for eighteen years, this Mac who I'd only seen bits and pieces of over the years, this Mac even I could be afraid of. I looked away as a quiet voice spoke behind us.

"That's enough, Andy. Your brother has enough nightmares." We turned and looked at Mac's mom. She stood looking down at the ground, flinching at the strap's cracking and Red's keening. She should've been used to the sounds, I thought. She heard them enough when Red whaled on Mac and Brad.

"Stop your brother, Andy."

Mac waited a couple of seconds, then nodded and caught Brad's arms on the upswing. Brad struggled in his grip, tears streaming down his face.

"Easy, easy now," Mac crooned as he pulled the strap out of Brad's hands and led him away from Red to the house. I looked at Mrs. MacAllister but, as usual, she refused to look me in the eye.

"Can Andy and Brad stay at your place for a while?" she asked. I nodded and, until Red's accident, Mac never went back home to stay. Brad left for his aunt's in Saskatoon when school let out and that's where he stayed. I'd kinda expected Mac to settle things with his dad next, but I guess the hate just wasn't as bad, that being neglected didn't eat at you like being beaten. Course Bill was probably happy that Mac had done something he'd never been able to. It was Mac's grandma, Mae, I felt sorry for. She had to go on living with old Red's anger. Never saw any bruises, but she wouldn't say boo even if Red wasn't around. She died six months after the fight, a small, timid woman who'd never had a chance to live outside Red's shadow.

I butted out my second smoke and listened to Benatar singing about hell being for children. No shit. Still no sign of Mac. Starter must be giving him more trouble than he'd expected. I lit another cigarette and wished I had a nice cold beer. I didn't even know what was wrong with Red now. I'd heard all the different rumours, that Red was dying, that he'd had a stroke, that he had Parkinson's disease, that he had this type or that type of cancer, or that he had Alzheimer's and couldn't remember Mac or Bill or anyone else's name half the time. Damned if I knew what the truth was. Mac and his dad generally couldn't agree on the time of day, but they'd agreed no one was allowed to see Red but family. This had put all of Pine Valley's old biddies out considerably, which was strange considering they never had a good word to say for Red in sixty-two years and would walk across the street if they saw him coming. Of course, anything that pissed off those old busybodies was good, I figured, but it would've been nice to know what the real story was, not the ones the crones made up. I popped the Benatar tape out and started flipping through the console for another. I looked up and saw Mac stomping out from among the cars. One look at his face and I decided we didn't need any party music. I left the radio on, playing some old sixties stuff.

Mac had the starter in one hand, his tool box in the other. He dropped the tool box by the corner of the office and held up a couple of fingers to me. "Two seconds while I pay for this."

"Whatever." I turned the key forward and the radio died. I got out, opened the hatch, and spread an old blanket over the floor. Glass clinked inside when I picked up Mac's tool box. A bottle? I frowned. It wasn't like Mac to sneak drinks like some old alky. This thing with Red was eating at him bad. His business, but his business had been my business since he was six and stayed over at our place for the first time to avoid a beating from Red when he was on the warpath. If I was lucky he'd talk about it in the bar after his visit with Red. I put the tool box on the blanket and looked at the office. Or maybe I had to push him. That was usually the only way to get to Mac. He came out of the office, and walked over, dropping the starter on the blanket.

"Jesus, Ken, you're worse than an old woman."

I shrugged. When you paid as much as I did for a car you took care of it. "As long as I don't start driving like one I don't care."

Mac just snorted and shook his head as we got into the car. "No fear of that."

"Where to?" I asked. He looked out the window, the muscles in his jaw tight under his reddening skin.

"Drop me off at the old folks' home and go get a beer. I won't be long."

"Okay." I backed the Mustang out, turned around and headed back into town. "How is old Red, anyway? Haven't seen him for over a year."

"Fine!"

I decided not to catch the hint, to live dangerously for a while. I flicked the radio off. "Yeah? Guess I'm curious, what with all the bullshit going around about him. You wouldn't believe what some of the old bags are saying."

"Shut the fuck up, Ken," he said edgily. His eyes were hard, angry, but the wildness wasn't there yet. I could push a little farther. But not too far. We'd had to stop Mac from beating on Nick Polanski after the stupid old shit got smashed and spouted off about Red being a vegetable. Of course, that was partly Mac and Bill's fault. They should know that if there was no story for the rumour mill, then somebody would make one up. Best way to head that off was to put out something of their own. Didn't have to be everything, just enough for the gossips to chew on.

"Why? I saw old Red almost as much as you did. Why the hell shouldn't I know how he is?"

"You're not family."

"Fuck you, Mac. I'm more your family than your old man ever was. I've been there – we've been there – for you a hell of a lot more than Red or Bill ever were. You want to pile that 'family' bullshit on me, then maybe you should think of all the nights you spent at our place, the times Mom and Dad fed you, the Christmas present for you under our tree. Think on all that, then give me that 'family' crap again."

Mac's face was brick red now, his lips a thin line, his eyes locked straight ahead. I waited for a reply, my grip tight on the wheel, pushing the gas pedal farther down. We whipped down the lane to the home, silent, memories and pride piling up between us. Gravel bouncing off the bottom of the car and the wind whistling through the open windows were the only sounds, the soundtrack to our twisted little movie. I ran lines through my head, bridges across the silence, but the anger kept them inside.

Finally the nursing home peeked out at us from the trees. We pulled into the parking lot, both of us staring straight ahead, neither of us wanting to speak first. The home was a long, low brick building, its trim a bright yellow against the green of the surrounding trees and lawn. A dozen types of flowers bloomed in the large flower beds in front of it and a high wooden fence encircled the back yard. Through a gate, I'd glimpsed a few old folks out on the patio as we drove up, but none of them looked like Red.

Mac had the door open before we even stopped. "Go get a beer. I'll be out here when you get back."

"Fuck you, Mac. I'm coming in." I don't know why I said it. It's not like I even liked old Red. And I sure the hell didn't like old folks' homes. Like feedlots. Bring them in, feed them, clean up their shit, then cart them out dead. I hoped someone would shoot me before they stuffed me in one. But I knew this wasn't about Red; it was about Mac. And you don't give up on your friends, no matter how much they deserve it sometimes.

"I told you, this is family business."

"Up yours. You know what I think of that family crap. Use it on me again and you're on your own. And you can explain to my folks how they're not family to you, you ungrateful bastard." I turned the car off, fought to calm myself. "I'm coming in whether you like it or not."

"Brant – Ken – "

"Shut up, Mac. I go in or we leave right now."

He stood half in, half out of the car. The anger was mostly gone from his face, replaced by confusion. And pain. Guess he didn't like to be on the receiving end of cheap shots. Tough. "Family," my ass. Finally he nodded. "Okay. But it stays between us."

I bit back my reply and nodded. I'd kept the MacAllister secrets all my life, it wasn't like I'd give the Pine Valley gossips anything now. We walked up the sidewalk and into the lobby.

The smell hit me first. Mr. Clean and Pinesol over smells I couldn't put words to, old people's smells, that kind of mouldy, slightly unclean smell that's more than shit or body odour. When I'd visited Great-Grandma I'd thought of it as the smell of death. It sure the hell wasn't any of the fresh smells that I thought of as life. This place was better than the home Gran had been in when I was a kid. Newer, brighter, a lot less dreary. Even the nurse at the desk was a different type. The one I remembered was lean and meaner than a cornered weasel. The one here was maybe fifty and fat, and her smile looked real. I bet she didn't bark orders like Nurse Weasel either.

"Hello, Andrew," she said. "How are you today?"

"Uh, fine." The hardness was gone from Mac's face and he looked ill at ease. "How's he doing today?"

"He was really good this morning, but he's slipped a bit this afternoon."

"Is he in his room?"

"Yes." She looked at me and smiled again. "Hi, I'm Rose." She stuck out her hand.

"Ken, Ken Brant." I gave her hand a quick shake. Mac was already heading down the hall, boots clicking on the linoleum as long strides carried him away. I started to follow when Rose spoke.

"Can you wait a minute, Ken?"

I looked at her, then after Mac.

"It's room 26," she said. I nodded, turned to face her, leaned on the high desk of the nursing station and raised my eyebrows in question.

"Are you a good friend of Andrew's?"

"Mac? His best friend."

She nodded, the smile gone from her face. "Does he talk about his grandfather much?"

"Nope. Mac isn't much of a talker." I hesitated, then decided I'd find out anyway. "Actually, I don't even know what's wrong with Red."

She frowned and shook her head. "We told the family not to keep it a secret. It's nothing to be ashamed of. Mr. MacAllister has Alzheimer's disease."

I took a deep breath, let it out in a rush. That had been one of the rumours, the most likely one, I'd figured. Parkinson's I would've noticed and a stroke or all the different cancers would've either been cured or killed him by now.

"How bad?" I asked.

"It's progressed fairly fast. He needs constant care now." She looked ill at ease. Probably worried about talking about family business. Then it hit me. She was worried about Mac too, could probably see the anger and pain that he always carried. But did she know the family? Did she know that Mac's mom hated Red, that Bill lived on the road to avoid Red, or that Mae had died in fear of her husband. Probably not. Like Mac said, that was family business. She'd know about the accident though, when Red had tried to use a chainsaw and ended up taking a big chunk out of his leg. He'd almost died before Mac found him.

"How long has he had it?"

"The progress varies from patient to patient but from what the family told us we think it started about five years ago.

Shit.

"Uh, I better see how Mac's doing." I started to move away from the counter before she could reply.

"Try to get him to talk," she said as I left the desk. "Keeping anger and pain inside like he does isn't healthy."

"Yeah, okay." I headed down the hallway. Maybe it wasn't healthy, but it was the only way Mac seemed to know, that his family seemed to know. Mac, Bill or Red, they could talk a blue streak, but it never amounted to shit. Brad was the only one who'd ever spoke about his dreams and look at all the grief it got him. If it wasn't for Mac, their mom, and my folks, the kid's life would've been an even worse hell that it was.

I stopped outside number twenty-six, my mouth dry. Alzheimer's. Shit. Red hadn't even made retirement age. I took a deep breath and knocked gently as I slowly opened the door.

"Mac?"

"Yeah, come in." I stepped into a small room looking out onto the backyard. The window was open and the scent of fresh-cut grass drifted into the room. Mac sat on the bed watching his grandfather look out the window. I stopped and despite myself, stared.

The old Red I remembered, the flaming-haired, deep-chested, booming-voiced tyrant sat slumped in a lounger, the thick red hair now grey wisps over a fish-white scalp, thin wrists sticking out of pajama sleeves. The huge hands that used to hold a belt or a bottle sat on the arms of the chair, skin tight over bone, translucent except for the liver spots. The eyes that glittered while Red told a story, or blazed when the temper was on him, were blank, unfocused, like they were on the day he'd stood in the yard, beaten. I felt pity wash over me, then remembered Red belittling his wife, terrorizing Mac and Brad, settling all of his problems with his fists, riding roughshod over anyone too weak to resist him. I remembered the bruises across my legs, Dad's eye swelling after he confronted Red, and the pity drained out of me. Nature had gotten what only Mac, out of all of us, had managed to get. Payback.

And payback was a bitch.

"Gramps, you remember Ken, Ken Brant? Arnold Brant's grandson? Ed Brant's son?"

"Of course I remember him. Used to bounce him on my knee while I had Andy on the other." He stared owlishly at Mac. "Andy, there was a good kid. Not a bookworm like Brad here. Still reading that faggy poetry, boy?"

Mac flushed. His hands started to clench into fists, then he straightened them. "Gramps, I am Andy."

"What?"

"I am Andy."

"What?"

Mac's face was beet red by now, but he didn't grab Red and shake him like I would've expected. And his voice was level. "Gramps, you're confused again. I am Andy."

"Andy was a good kid. Hell of a hockey player. Good scrapper too. Always getting kicked out of the game, but he always came out on top." He chuckled and some life came back into his eyes. "That kid was a stubborn little fucker. Saw him get pitched eight times first time he rode a horse and he got back on every fucking time. Outstubborned a Shetland pony."

Mac's face had lost most of the red. "Yeah, I did, didn't I?" A smile flitted across his face and I looked at him in disbelief. I remembered the fear in his eyes that day and it wasn't of the horse, it was of Red. Red had sat on the fence at Radinski's yelling at Mac. "Don't be a girl," and "Be a man," and "Get back on that horse, you're a MacAllister. Act like it." Mac had hid the tears of pain that day. After all, the bruises weren't nearly as bad as the ones he got from Red.

"Yeah, a stubborn little shit. Needed to beat on him regular. Only way he was going to come out normal, not like that no-good father of his. Fuck anything that walks, that useless little prick. Probably got blow jobs at half the truck stops in Canada. The States too. All he ever thought of, that boy, his cock and where he could stick it. Eighteen years old and he already had one girl knocked up. Couldn't be easy on that kid like I was on his dad. Couldn't make the same mistake twice." He looked out the window and shook his head. "He was a good kid, Andy was. Wild, but not like Bill or Brad. Wish he'd come and see me sometime."

Mac's shoulders were slumped, shrinking into himself. His eyes were closed but I could see the pain on his face.

"Mac?"

"Not now." He straightened and looked at his grandfather, something that could have been caring on his face. Jesus, he had to be crazier than the old man. How could he forget the strap? And the stupid rules, changing whenever Red got another bright idea? A few stupid stories and he was forgetting that? Well I wasn't. Not now. Not ever.

"Gramps, what else can you remember about me? About Andy? Do you remember more about that time at Radinski's?"

"Radinski. Fucking Bohunk. Cocksuckers took over the country when they moved in." He chuckled. "Bunch of big men. Showed them what was what when they tried to take over one of our dances before the war. Tried sparking my girl so I took the single tree off the wagon and went after the bastards. Polacks and Ukes running every which way." He smiled at the memory. "The Bohunks learned not to mess with Red MacAllister that night."

Mac chuckled. "I bet they did, Gramps." He didn't look my way. Lucky he didn't have Radinski or Darchuk along. They would've loved that story. Red was still smiling to himself, lost in some past that was clearer to him than anything recent, anything that mattered to Mac.

"Do you want to go outside, Gramps?"

"What?"

"Do you want to go outside?"

"What's there outside?"

"Nothing. Just the sunshine and some fresh air."

"Fresh air? Why?"

"I just thought you'd like it, Gramps."

"Why?"

"Jesus, Mac," I said. Mac spun towards me, face reddening again.

"I told you to shut the fuck up before. You too stupid to remember?"

"Fuck you." I got up and looked at Red, at the confusion on his face, and still couldn't feel any pity. "It's been a slice, Red," I said, turning and walking to the door, stopping when Red spoke.

"Come back and see me sometime, Ken. I don't get many visitors." I closed my eyes, steeling myself against the sudden, unexpected rush of emotion.

"Yeah, Red, I'll do that." I stepped out before he could say anything more.

"That Ken is a good kid. Never had much speed, but what a shot. Pick the..." The closing door cut the rest off and I leaned against the wall, shivering. The fucking twilight zone, that's what this day had become. What planet was Red on? And why the hell had Mac joined him there? I stood against the wall for long minutes, letting my heart and breathing slow, twisting what I'd just seen every which way, trying to find a way that made sense. Finally I gave up and walked down to the nurses' station. Rose sat watching me, a chart forgotten in front of her.

"How damn long has this been going on?" I asked harshly.

"Andrew's been visiting since shortly after his grandfather was transferred here from the hospital."

"His name is Mac. You're not his grandma so why do you call him Andrew?"

She looked at me steadily, the smile off her face but her eyes still warm. "He asked me to."

"What?" Mac had barely tolerated Mae calling him Andrew. Why – Oh Christ. I took another look at Rose. The hair was close to the same colour, and she was about the same size, but that was it. Mae she was not. Or at least to me. She looked at me, eyes steady, no fear in them. Definitely not Mae. I took a deep breath.

"Sorry," I said. "This whole thing is a little too weird."

"Why? Is it so wrong for a grandson to love his grandfather?"

"Love? They're MacAllisters. They wouldn't know love for one another if it jumped up and bit them on the ass."

"You're so sure? You could be wrong, you know. Emotions aren't that easy to figure out. You get a bit older and you realize that."

"Yeah, right," I said, getting as much sarcasm as I could into my voice. I might only be nineteen, but I knew a lot more than she thought. "Did Mac ever tell you about his childhood? No? Then let me fill you in." I gave it all to her, the beatings, the fight, Red's belittling them, Bill's slutting around and resentment of Mac, everything. She nodded a lot and asked few questions. Not that there'd be much to ask. It was cut and dried, after all. When I was done, I felt wrung out. She handed me a Coke from under the counter. It was warm, but my throat didn't care.

"I had a picture something like that built up," she said, "from the things Red said, but I didn't know it was that bleak. Red always talks about horses and hockey games and ball games and..."

"And what? Drinking and fighting?" She nodded. "Yeah, well that was about all the old prick knew. If Mac did them well, he had a shot at not getting whaled on. If not, he was fu – screwed." She wasn't Mae, but I had been letting my anger control my language. "Anyway, Mac can't care for him. You don't just dump twenty years of hate because someone gets sick."

"No, but you can find other things that the hate was hiding."

"Like what?"

"Like being at all his ball games and hockey games –"

"Half in the bag most of the time."

"And he bought him a horse."

"That would buck him off or kick him every chance it got."

"And he was there all the times Andrew's father wasn't."

"Because Pine Valley is the perfect small pond to be a big fish in."

"You won't give him any credit, will you?"

"Credit is earned, just like trust. Even a nineteen-year-old knows that."

"But forgiveness is freely given. Or at least it is if it means anything." She looked at me, worry and warmth fighting for space in her eyes.

"Spare me the pop psychology."

She shook her head sadly. "What made you so cynical so young?"

"Life." Life and Pine Valley. That was the problem with a small town, the only way you could avoid the unpleasant parts of life was to pretend they didn't exist or to get so wrapped up in your life that you couldn 't see outside your own yard. And I'd pretended with Mac and his family too long.

"Why did you come here then, if you didn't want to see Red?"

Damn. She was smart. Guess I wasn't the only one who'd seen a bit of life. And she'd had more time and opportunity to see the worst in people. And the best.

"To see what was bugging Mac."

"So you're not too cynical to help a friend."

"No. Just too confused." We stopped talking as we heard Mac's boots clicking down the hallway. He walked by us without a word, face set and blazing red. He straight-armed the front door open and stalked out to the Mustang. I followed him as far as the front door and watched him reach under the wheel well and get the magnetic case that held my spare keys. The hatch obscured what he was doing when he got it open, but I knew. He slammed it down, waved angrily at me and plopped himself in the front seat. He didn't even try to hide the twenty-six as he chugged at it, his Adam's apple bobbing up and down. I looked at Rose, who had followed me to the door, and shrugged.

"It must be tough loving and hating someone at the same time," she said. "He needs a friend now, more than ever."

I nodded. "And if I can't bring him back?"

"Then Andrew has got a hard life ahead of him."

"Don't we all," I said, as I pushed through the door. "Don't we all."

Mac said nothing as I got in, just handed me the bottle when I put my hand out. The whisky burned comfortably as I took a large swallow. I handed it back to Mac and started the car, saying nothing. This had to be at his pace. We crept out of the parking lot, things even more strained than when we'd arrived. I headed the Mustang slowly down the road, waiting, praying, for Mac to speak. A Lincoln pulled up behind us as we putted along, horn blaring impatiently. A straw hat bobbed up and down above the wheel. I watched the old guy in the rear-view mirror for a while, then pulled over. He sailed by, his land ark whisper-silent. Gravel bounced off the windshield, the only sound except for the swish of the rye as Mac swigged at it. We drove in silence, the Lincoln moving farther and farther away, finally disappearing.

Mac didn't say a word the whole way home.

DEAR
PENTHOUSE

Women deprived of the company of men pine,
men deprived of the company of women become stupid.
— ANTON CHEKHOV

I could hear Mac and Wayne arguing as soon as I left the last bunk car. I stopped on the platform and listened for a second. Same old bullshit, this time the *Penthouse* argument, so I leaned on the railing to enjoy the sunset for awhile.

The sun was a huge orange ball sinking below the horizon. We got a lot more spectacular sunsets in Saskatchewan, especially in spring and fall, when there were all sorts of reds and yellows in the evening sky and every one was different. Here in northern Manitoba in July the sunsets were all the same and all too damn late in the evening. What made them special was the way the sunlight would wash over the mile after mile of stunted pine that made up everything we could see, relieving it of its monotony and softening its harshness. The land looked inviting, like people ought to be here.

Of course that impression only lasted for a few minutes, then you remembered what kind of shithole the rail line to Churchill really was.

I shook my head. Two and a half weeks up north and already I was getting bushed. I opened the door to the recreation car and walked in. Radinski and Darchuk were playing kaiser against Nelson and Grier while Mac sat at a table with the Dupuis brothers arguing over an issue of *Penthouse*. A typical evening on the railroad in nowhere Manitoba.

"Of course they're not real," Wayne Dupuis said, referring to the letters in *Penthouse*. "I bet they got some guy who sits there and that's his job, to think up all these wild letters. That's why they all sound the same after a while."

"They sound like that because the guys that send them in don't know how to tell a really good story," Mac said. "They just use the same bullshit they've read before. I mean, look at this." He picked up the magazine and began to read. "I pulled out my ten inches and her eyes widened. 'What a whopper,' she said." He threw the magazine down. "It's a whopper all right, a whopper some guy thought up at home, not in some office."

"What, you don't have a ten-inch dick?" Wayne's brother, Louis, asked. We all laughed as he grabbed his crotch. "Standard equipment on us Dupuis."

Mac sneered at Louis. "And it pumps out gallons every time you come?"

"Of course," Wayne said. He picked up another *Penthouse*. "Here's why I know these things are written by some poor guy locked up in an office somewhere jerking off six times a day." He read, "'I pulled out my foot-long hot dog and she swooned.' Who the hell says 'swooned'? Some university type who's been doing this for too long, that's who."

"Maybe," Mac said. "Why don't we ask the Professor?" We all turned and looked at Nelson. He was our resident brain, an English major at the University in Saskatoon.

"Don't put me in the middle of this," Nelson said. "We had this argument last year, Wayne. We never did come to an agreement."

"Yeah, but you got to agree with one of us."

Nelson looked from Mac to Wayne, then back again. He smiled, shoving himself up from where he was slouched in the wooden chair. He pulled his shoulders back and rolled his neck. I smiled. It was time for a visit from the Professor.

"Content analysis of the material reveals common roots in the subject matter," he said in a nasal English accent. "Whether these roots are mythic, based on exaggerated folk tales, or on the works of Henry Miller is a matter of conjecture. What is known is that the limited number of themes and repeated use of a limited number of tropes suggests that there has been extensive cross-fertilization and borrowing in the form leading to a formulaic sameness bordering on the development of a stylized art form akin to an O. Henry short story with its twist endings." He stopped and said in his normal voice, "And that's all I've got to say about that."

Everyone looked at Grier, then at me. Grier waved his hand at me.

"You explain it Ken," he said. "I'm just a poor engineer who squeaked through his Arts classes."

And I was just a nineteen-year-old who read a lot. Still, this was easier than most of the Professor's pronouncements.

"I don't know what the Henry Miller thing is all about, but the rest means it's the same old bullshit over and over again," I said. Nelson smiled and touched his index finger to his nose before picking his cards up again. I shook my head. That's why we got along with Nelson, because he didn't take himself or all his schooling too seriously. A couple of the other college types did, but they didn't hang around with us.

"Why the hell didn't you just say so," Wayne said, chuckling. "And you can't tell me people really talk like that."

Nelson and Grier looked at each other. Grier nodded.

"I'll be dipped in shit," Wayne said. "And here I thought you were just fucking with us poor country boys' heads last year."

Nelson shook his head as he looked at his cards. "Nope. Though this year I'd be tempted to if I figured it'd pass the time quicker." He looked at the other three players. "Do you really care if we finish this game?"

Ski's response was to throw his cards in, followed half a second later by Darchuk and Grier.

"I think we'd all like something to make the time go quicker," Ski said, "but we've done pretty much everything there is to do the last little while."

No shit, I thought. Card games, tournaments,

shuffleboard, drinking, smoking pot, we'd done it all and still had too much spare time. Even we readers were finding we'd overestimated the amount of time we could spend with our nose in a book. Especially when the rest of the guys were hovering around trying to fill time. I looked at the television shoved into the corner. Lot of good it did up here. And the Betamax under it was as useful as a boat anchor since our section foreman always forgot to bring tapes with him from Winnipeg.

I missed TV. I'd even sit through an episode of *The Beachcombers* right now. I looked at the book in my hands. *Heart of Darkness* by Joseph Conrad. Nelson had lent it to me, told me it was the best book ever written. He definitely needed to learn what a good book was if he really believed that.

Mac was skimming through the *Penthouse*, a big, shit-eating grin on his face. "I've got an idea," he said. "How about we have a contest to see who can write the best letter."

Smiles appeared and heads started nodding throughout the room.

"I'll be damned," Wayne said, "something we never tried last year."

"And something you guys might have a slight chance of beating us at," Grier said to a chorus of boos and fuck offs.

"College boys," Wayne said, shaking his head. "No way you can tell a story better than us Metis. We've got storytelling in our blood." He pursed his lips. "Though I doubt Louis Riel or Gabriel Dumont ever told a story with 'Fuck me, big boy,' in it."

"You sure?" Mac said as we laughed. "You never know what kind of bullshit went around the campfire when a buffalo was the best-looking thing in fifty miles."

"That's a couple of hundred miles closer to the nearest woman than we are," Radinski said. "Unless you count Esther and Flora."

"You can count them, Ski," Wayne said, "but if those two start looking good to me I'm on the first train south."

We all nodded. Esther and Flora were our two assistant cooks. They were nice enough women, but both over fifty and over two hundred and fifty pounds. I was having a hard time wrestling hormones but if things got that desperate I wasn't waiting for the train, I was running all the way south.

"Who's going to judge this thing and what are the rules?" Grier asked.

"Rules? Have you read the letters?" Wayne said. "Only things they don't have in them is animals and dead people and who wants to hear about that anyway?"

"Okay, but what about team size and the time limit?" Grier asked.

"Christ, Grier, pull the stick out of your ass. You gotta have a rule for everything?" Wayne said.

"Forgive him," Nelson said before Grier could reply. "Engineers tend to be a bit anal-retentive about details. How about four people per team, fifteen minutes each, and we do the reading on Sunday. Only a nine-hour day, then, and no overtime so we can get the rest of the gang out to watch and judge."

"Who do we get for judges?" Grier asked.

We spent the next ten minutes tossing names

around before settling on Curtis, our cook, Warren, our youngest assistant foreman and Tony, our Sicilian crane operator. Curtis and Warren would both laugh at this, we figured, and Tony was the undisputed storytelling champ in the camp. He'd sit down with Wayne and Mac and away they'd go. Mac kept up pretty good, considering he was ten years younger than Wayne and twenty-five years younger than Tony, but Tony had his Mafia stories to top the other two.

"We going to make this interesting?" Mac asked.

"Sure." Wayne shrugged. "Twenty bucks each, winning team takes the pot?"

We all nodded and then Mac looked at his watch.

"Bedtime for this cowboy. That goddamn sledgehammer is waiting for me tomorrow and all I'll dream about tonight is swinging the damn thing."

We got up to leave. I tossed the book on the table in front of Nelson.

"If that's the best you've got I'm going to have to actually read the stories in the skin magazines."

"You don't think it's a classic?" Nelson said.

"Only if you mean boring, like classical music. Some of the bits on the trip were good, but it took way too long to get to the good stuff with Kurtz."

"Everyone's a critic," he said. "Best I can do, though. All I brought are classics and if you don't like Conrad, then Joyce isn't going to do it for you."

"I've got a book for you," Grier said. "And it's interesting."

"Yeah?" I wasn't sure about this. Grier had never struck me as much of a reader. "What's it about?"

"A mad bomber that blows up buildings."

"Sounds good," I said half-heartedly. Nelson had said *Heart of Darkness* was about a Company man who goes into Africa after a rogue operative. I'd thought he meant CIA when he said Company, so like a starving fish I took the bait. Grier could be doing the same. Still, beggars can't be choosers, so I said, "I'll pick it up tomorrow after work."

"Is the book any good?" Mac asked, his attention on the joint he was rolling.

"Better than the last one," I said, putting down *The Fountainhead*, "but the bastards did it to me again. I had to skim through to near the end to find anything about someone blowing up buildings."

"You going to take them messing with your head or do we kick their asses in this letter thing?"

I snapped the book shut. "Let's kick some University butt." I pulled open the bottom drawer on our closet and dug out our stash of skin magazines from under my woodworking magazines. I separated the *Penthouse* from the *Swank,* the *Oui* and all the rest, then handed Mac half the stack.

"Let's go through them with a fine-tooth comb and see what we find."

"That content analysis stuff Nelson talked about? That's – " Mac was interrupted by a knock on the door. He shoved the joint and the Baggie full of pot under his pillow, then answered it.

"Let's get this fucking letter done," Ski said as he

walked in. He dropped onto Mac's bed and I sat up so Darchuk could sit on the end of mine. I tilted my head toward Ski and looked at Darchuk. He grimaced and mouthed the word "Wayne." I nodded. Ski had been yapping a lot when we hit camp about how many women he'd had and how good they all were. We'd put up with it for a couple of years in Pine Valley, but Wayne had cut the legs out from under Ski, mocking him anytime he got going. "Hey guys, did you know Radinski invented sex?" "Louis, you ever get a blow job from a woman who could suck a golf ball through a garden hose?" Ski had finally learned to keep his mouth shut around Wayne, so the rest of us had followed Wayne's example. Anything to keep Ski quiet. His bullshit was fine in small doses but it got old real quick when we were seeing each other every day.

"Nice to see you're ready to go, Ski," Mac said, firing the joint up. He took a deep drag, then handed it to Ski who took a hit and handed it to Darchuk. Mac let the smoke out.

"I suppose you want to use one of your stories so you can rub Wayne's nose in it?" he said.

"Fucking right, I do."

"That could be a problem," Mac said. "Piling bullshit on top of bullshit doesn't make for the best story. It's like building a house on permafrost; it's going to sink under its own weight."

"You saying I'm a liar?"

"No," Mac said mildly, much to my relief. Mac was always ready for a fight and Ski's reputation as a stud was the kind of sore point that could get Ski swinging.

Good thing pot mellowed us. Even Mac. "Relax, Ski," Mac said. "It's just you don't know how to tell a story well, is all."

Ski opened his mouth, then closed it. If anyone knew how to tell a story well, it was Mac. Learned it at his grandfather's knee. Nobody beat Red MacAllister at storytelling. Before the Alzheimer's got him, he would've blown Tony out of the water as fast as Tony did Mac, with stories from the forties and fifties, back when things were still in the horse stage for a lot of Pine Valley. Or his war stories. His stories didn't have the Mafia in them, but Red had made things sound a hell of a lot more impressive. He used to make you feel like you were there.

"You've got to have something real to build on, something to embellish, as Nelson would say. That's why we have to have our best sex in this letter. And don't be shy, by the time we're done no one will recognize anybody."

We sat silently, thinking for a couple of minutes while Mac rolled another joint. It was homegrown shit we bought off one of the train's brakemen and it took a couple of joints to have any effect. Floor sweepings at Acapulco Gold prices. Our sex lives? Two twenty-year-olds, Darchuk still a few weeks from his twentieth, and me not turning twenty until October. Not like we had a huge pile of experience, except for Ski, and even most of those weren't anything special, or were him trying to make the score more impressive. I'd been with all of three women and only one seriously, Darchuk something similar, Mac maybe a couple more and Ski probably a few more than that, though he claimed way over ten. Not a huge base to work from.

The second joint went around the room. Ski reached up and slid the window open to let the smell of the pot out. Our foremen didn't make much of an effort to catch anyone drinking or using, but why rub their noses in it. Finally Ski broke the silence.

"You're the one with the bright idea, Mac, so why don't you go first?"

"Quit pouting, Ski, I just made a comment. Not everyone can be a great storyteller, that's all."

"Then tell us about your best lay, O great fucking storyteller." Ski took an extra large hit off the joint, the blood still up in his face.

"Okay, it was with Donna Unger. We – " Mac stopped as I shook my head at him. He never knew when to quit. It was too late though.

"Fuck, MacAllister, why do you always have to bring that up? You rub Greg's nose in it all the time and I'm sick of it. Besides, Donna said nothing happened, especially not the blow job."

"That's her story. I'm trying to tell you mine."

"Shut up, Mac," I said, trying to stop things from getting totally out of hand. Donna was Radinski's best friend's fiancée and she and Mac had gone out for the last few months of high school. Only time Donna went out with anybody besides Greg Hicks. It had been pretty intense to hear Mac tell it, but he'd gone too far the way he bragged about it and ended up driving Donna right back to Hicks. Now Donna and Hicks were getting married next summer and Ski was best man. Mac definitely wasn't invited to the wedding.

"But – "

"I said shut up!" If Ski started in on him, Mac would just get more and more defensive, and that would mean an ugly argument, the kind nobody won.

"Yeah, Mac, keep quiet," Ski said, "because if you use Donna, then Ken has to tell us about Trish."

"Kiss my ass! You – " I was leaning forward, ready to really blast Ski, when Darchuk put a hand on my chest and pushed me back.

"This is bullshit," he snapped. "I know we're all getting bush fever but is this stupid contest worth ripping up our friendship for?" He looked at Mac. "Is it that important that you beat Wayne? Same for you, Ski?"

"No, but we're just talking about sex, not something important," Mac said. "Christ, it's not like we've talked about much else since we got here."

Darchuk shook his head, Ski nodded in agreement with Mac. I was with Darchuk on this one. Sure you talked about sex, but not when it mattered. Trish and I had gone out together for a year and a half before I got her pregnant last year. We'd moved in together for a couple of weeks before she'd miscarried. I'd fallen in love with her, but we hadn't been able to survive the strain of losing the baby. Be damned if I was going to talk about that. Darchuk had had something happen with a woman last summer when he and Ski were working in Alberta but he never talked about it and Ski wouldn't say anything. Only thing I knew was that Darchuk just about failed out of university at Christmas. Ski had gone down to Saskatoon after that and dragged Darchuk out to some parties. Darchuk got laid and Ski figured that took care of everything, since a piece of tail cured all that ailed you, right?

Wrong.

"Fine," Darchuk was saying, "if we're supposed to talk about sex, then we talk about Ski and his twenty-five-year-old." It was wild sex that Ski loved talking about. "Or we take something somebody else had happen and dress it up. We don't talk about Donna or Trish or anybody else we don't want to talk about. Otherwise, I'm out of here."

"Me too," I said. Fucking Radinski, he didn't know the difference between fucking and making love. I shot him a dirty look and he had the decency to look away sheepishly.

"Fine," Mac said. "Christ, try to do things right and everyone jumps all over you."

"So do something with Ski's story," Darchuk said. "You're the storyteller. Make it work."

Mac nodded. "I can do that." He looked at Ski. "I need all the details. And I mean every single one."

Ski smiled and started talking.

The rain started just after supper the next day. It drummed on the tin roof of the bunk car as we settled into our room again. Mac had the joints ready to go and the *Penthouse*s piled up on the table. I wrinkled my nose as he fired up the first one. None of us were into pot that much, but we drank the booze we smuggled up here the first week and we only managed a couple of nights straight before we were pooling our cash and joining the lineup to the baggage car of the freight train. Don't think it was one of the supplies the foremen expected in camp, but it kept us quiet in the evening. Only reason they didn't catch everyone, I figured. Hard enough to find people to work up here. We'd already had half a dozen quit and a lot more were unhappy. We had a little piece of Pine Valley here so things were a bit easier for the four of us.

"Okay, guys," Mac said, "we need to find the letters that'd give a hard-on to a statue and see why they work, then use that to write our letter. We've got something to build on, but we need to give it the right spin."

"I thought you said that wouldn't work?" I said.

"I said it wouldn't work if that's all we did."

"So you want the hottest or what they do the most of?" I said.

"Maybe the most first," Mac said. "They wouldn't print a bunch of them if they didn't figure they were surefire dick stiffeners."

"That's easy then," Darchuk said. "Lots of group scenes, two women, one man, tag teaming a woman and her loving it, uh – "

"Women wanting a huge cock and just begging for it," I said.

"Young babysitters doing the man of the house," Ski tossed in.

"Or the couple," Darchuk said.

"A couple of young babysitters," "with tight little bodies," "doing everything a guy could ever want," "twice," "and with each other."

"Enough already," Mac said, shaking his head and smiling. "Guess we don't have to read them again. Got the things memorized."

"No kidding," Ski said. "Other guys are going to be like us so they'll probably think of the same ideas. How're we going to spin ours to make it better than theirs?"

"Same thing I said last night before we started ripping each other's heads off," Mac replied. "We've got to use everything we can to make it seem real, and figure out what works in the magazine but won't work when I'm telling the story."

"Such as?" I asked. This was the most interest I'd seen Mac take in anything and it was the happiest he'd been since his grandfather, Red, had ended up in a nursing home with Alzheimer's and his family had scattered, leaving just him and his dad on the farm. Probably because he figured he was doing something Red would've liked and was getting a chance to beat Wayne in the bargain.

"Well, I can't tell the story like I'm a woman writing it, and that takes care of probably half the letters."

"Too bad," Ski said. "Some of those are really hot."

"Maybe," Mac said, "but no way am I reading 'I moaned as he stuffed his big tool into me.'"

We laughed. "Okay, okay," I said, "that doesn't work, but what else can't we use?"

"Anything that sounds like it's not me talking. I can't nail a babysitter unless it's someone else's babysitter because I don't have any kids, I can't end up with some classy businesswoman type unless her car breaks down in Pine Valley, the guys have seen me in the shower car so I can't pretend I have a ten-inch dick that I tease some woman with while she begs for it." He stopped and frowned. "Christ, that knocks out a lot of them, doesn't it?"

"Uh-huh." I looked at Mac in amazement. He'd been quiet all day, and he'd bounced ideas off Darchuk at lunch but he was way past us on how we could actually win this thing.

"Jeez, Mac, if they do have some guy sitting in an office writing these things you'd be a shoo-in for the job," Ski said.

"Of course," Mac said. "It's all just storytelling and I'm the best there is."

"Would you like to be alone with your ego?" Darchuk asked. "You could get as annoying as Ski, you keep that up." Ski shot Darchuk a dirty look, which he ignored.

Mac smiled. "Nah. I'll only be annoying to the Dupuis boys when we win. And maybe Grier."

"Great, but we have to win first," I said. Picking Grier's ass would be fun, but we couldn't underestimate Nelson. Could only hope university had screwed up his ability to tell a story that would click with a bullshitter like Tony. He'd know enough not to use a word like *swooned* but could he keep it on the same level as the rest of us?

"One way we're a bit ahead of Wayne or Nelson is that I look a lot closer to the way the guys in the letters describe themselves than those two do," Mac said.

"A lot?" Ski said, raising one eyebrow.

"Yeah, a lot," Mac said. "Christ, Nelson looks like a blond Q-tip and that gut on Wayne sure isn't like anything in the letters. And he waddles when he walks."

I looked at Darchuk and saw him bite his lip too. Sure Mac was six foot two and in good shape, but he'd never win any beauty contests. He had the most godawful case of permanent windburn and his skin never tanned to brown, it just got redder. And then there were the freckles. No, if we were picking our storyteller on looks, Mac wouldn't win.

Of course, the rest of us wouldn't win any prizes either. Ski came the closest. He was as tall as Mac, and more muscular. I'd even heard women call him rugged, but the fish-belly-white forehead we all had from our hardhats worked against him, as did the five o'clock shadow he'd had since he was sixteen. And Darchuk and I were both average sized and hadn't had to spend a lot of time beating the women off with a stick. No, this was definitely *not* going to be a beauty contest.

"Anyways," Mac said, "here's the way I start. I meet the woman in the bar and she's hot. We make the clothes she's wearing a lot sluttier than what she was really wearing, to show she's out looking to get laid. We get the old crotches grinding when we dance and she takes me by the hand and yanks me out of the bar. We're all over each other before we even get to the car and we start with a blow job in the parking lot. That should take the first five minutes or so, then we can really heat things up."

"Sounds good so far, but can you spice it up in the bar? A lot of them start in the bar after all," I said.

"And the parking lot thing isn't new," Darchuk said. He leafed through one of the *Penthouse*s, stopped, then read for a few seconds. "Thought so. A woman going down on her cab driver before he gives her his big tip."

"You ever get head in a car?" Ski said. "Think it happens every day?"

Darchuk looked at Ski coldly, head cocked to one side. Ski grimaced.

"Okay, stupid question," he said. "But we've got to start somewhere and I'm sure nobody else will have anything that isn't in one of the letters already. It's impossible."

"And my idea is better than anything I've heard from you jerk-offs so far," Mac said. He frowned at Darchuk. "If you had something so exciting last year why don't you tell us about it. Or maybe it was nothing special and you're just trying to make us think something happened with this big silent act."

"What happened last year is none of your business, Mac."

"If you're going to be a tight-ass, why should we listen to your ideas?"

"I guess you're right." Darchuk stood up. "This whole letter thing is stupid. I don't need bragging rights over Wayne or Grier, so I'm out of here." He stepped toward the door.

"So you slept with a married woman," Mac said, stopping Darchuk dead in his tracks. "Big deal. My dad nails married women all the time. Figures they're easier to dump that way. They can't make a big fuss like a single woman might."

"How – " Darchuk glared at Ski, who held his hands up defensively.

"I'm not stupid," Mac said. "Figured it out a while ago that that could be the only thing you and Ski wouldn't talk about."

"It's still none of your business!"

"Christ, you've got the best story of all of us, something that might be a bit new and real, and you sit there saying nothing."

"Back off, Mac," I said, seeing Darchuk's fists clenching.

"Yah, Mac, let it go," Ski said.

Confused, Mac looked around at all of us. "What the hell is the big deal? You think I'm going to tell anyone in Pine Valley? You nuts? None of their business, and I wouldn't give all the gossips there the sweat off my balls."

Darchuk relaxed a bit at that, but he still didn't sit down.

"C'mon, Eric, we're not in Pine Valley anymore. Your family isn't going to find out."

"No? Four of us know what happened now. You figure nobody will get hammered some day and let things slip out? Or get close to some woman and tell her?"

"Sit down, Eric," Mac said softly. "Did you hear me say a word about Ken and Trish? Or has Ski said a thing about you and this woman? And Ken has never talked about any of the things he's seen out at my place. We all know how to keep secrets."

"You've got to promise," Darchuk said, sitting down. "This would kill Mom and Dad if they ever found out."

Mac and I both promised.

"Okay," Darchuk said. "I still don't want to use her in this stupid contest though."

"It would be a winner," Mac said. He held up a hand to stop Darchuk's protest. "Relax. It was just an observation. Still, I don't think you know how bad I want to win this thing."

"Why? It's just a stupid game."

"It's my game. I thought of the idea and I can taste winning it." He thought for a few seconds. "Guess the only way to explain it is to use Ski. You know how noisy you are on the ball diamond, how pissed off you get when we lose, well that's me whenever Wayne tops me with a better story. He screws up here and there and still it's better because he's got such great material. I've got to start farther back. This letter thing puts me even with him. I won't have to walk out of the rec car and end up staring at the ceiling figuring out ways I could've told the story better to beat him."

Darchuk nodded. Longest speech I'd ever heard Mac make. Ski was probably just about as pumped for the contest, but I didn't care that deeply and Darchuk wasn't too enthusiastic either. Not when he was the one whose sex life would be on display.

"How about losing to Tony?" Ski said. "Why doesn't that piss you off?"

"He's got perfect timing and great material. Him topping me is like our ball team losing to the Blue Jays; you just don't feel that bad, because winning would be a miracle."

We nodded. Mac pulled out his stash and started

rolling another joint. "Tell you what. I'll think on the letter tomorrow and try to give you guys something closer to the way I'll tell it. Then you can see how it's not like the other letters we've read."

"Okay," I said, " but what does that leave the rest of us to do?" I looked at my watch. Eight-thirty. "And what can we do to kill the rest of the evening? That was the point of this whole thing wasn't it, to give us all something to do?"

"No reason we can't write another letter," Mac said. "Anybody ever dream of nailing one of the Bertrand sisters? Or all of them at once?"

I smiled. There were six Bertrand sisters, each more beautiful than the last and each disgustingly faithful to the long-term boyfriends they seemed to acquire. Still, for the last ten years, every guy in Pine Valley had had fantasies about them.

"Mac, you can't have all six of them at once," Ski said. "It's physically impossible."

"And greedy," Darchuk added.

The next letter flowed out.

Ski was sitting at one of the tables in the dining car drinking coffee when I came in the next morning. The car was only a third full, with Jake, the assistant foreman, and a couple of other guys sitting at the same table as Ski. Wayne, Louis and the rest of their group sat at a table at the other end of the car. Nobody said anything, just choked down what passed for breakfast and chugged back coffee. They muttered hello when I sat down, but that was it. None of us had any energy in the morning, especially since we got up north.

The toast was cold, but I slathered peanut butter and jam on it and crunched through it, softening it with coffee before I swallowed. Tony and the other guys started getting up, heading for their rooms to get their rain gear and hard hats. Weather up here meant six layers of clothes in the morning, a T-shirt and insect repellant by noon and a jean jacket in the evening. God's country it wasn't.

"Where's Mac?" Ski asked, when the others had left. He said it quietly, like he was worried Wayne and the rest might be listening, or cared what we were talking about.

"Still sleeping."

"Yeah, right. Probably spanking the monkey."

"Darchuk?"

"The same."

I nodded. I missed weekends at home in my own room. I missed parties, where women smiled at me and there was at least a hope of more. I looked at Flora as she came to clean up the other guy's plates. Still not looking good. I'd stay another day.

Wayne and the others got up. Wayne had his usual toothpick in the corner of his mouth. Don't think I ever saw him without one. He smiled when he saw us.

"If it ain't the competition. Ready to get your asses whipped, boys."

"We'll see who gets their asses whipped," I said.

"Sure you will," Wayne said. "You've got Radinski on your team after all, the Man Who Invented Sex himself.

How can you lose?" He looked at Ski and laughed.

I kicked Ski's leg under the table as he started to get up. He ignored me. "Care to make it really interesting? How about you and me, a hundred bucks apiece."

"Make it two. My kids' teeth need work."

I looked at Louis even though he never had much control over his younger brother. Still, he was the calm one. He nodded at me.

"A hundred is enough, Wayne," he said. "And the yapping stops after Sunday."

"Not if I win," Wayne said.

"Fair enough," Ski said, " but be ready for me in your face when we stomp you."

"Yeah, I – " Wayne was cut short as Louis dropped a large hand on his shoulder and squeezed. He turned his head and glared but Louis just smiled at him unperturbed. Finally Wayne relaxed.

"Later guys," Louis said, steering Wayne out the door. I nodded.

"Fucking asshole," Ski said.

"Don't let him get to you. Laugh him off."

"No, I want back at him."

"Then work with Mac on the letter."

He nodded. "You want to work on the auto-spiker today? I want to swap ideas with Mac." He smiled. "And hammer a few spikes I imagine Wayne's face on."

Trade swinging a sledgehammer all day for moving a couple of levers while sitting down? There was a no-brainer.

"No problem," I said.

That night we met in Ski and Darchuk's room. Mac looked manic and Ski wasn't much better. Darchuk rolled his eyes. You'd think we were playing in the Grey Cup or something.

"You got it figured out finally?" I asked.

"Yeah." Mac took the joint from Ski and took a hit. "We're going to cheat a bit."

"There's no rules so how can we cheat?"

"We're supposed to write the best *Penthouse* letter. That sticks us with doing the same old bullshit they do. Never takes any time to get into the girl's pants, she's always ready to do anything, and lots of times there's a whole crew doing it at once. That's not how it usually happens."

"So?" Ski said.

"Everyone knows that," I said.

"What's your point?" said Darchuk.

Mac's forehead furrowed and he shook his head at the three of us.

"That is the point. I want to tell the story the way I would in the bar, the way that's hottest."

We looked at each other. Ski looked totally confused, but I thought I knew where Mac was going with this.

"What's the difference?" Ski asked.

"For you, not much, because you cut right to the chase. Me, I'd build it up, let everyone get a picture of what I was doing, work in little details to let the other guys think they're there. And I'd build things up slowly, bringing the audience into the story."

I thought about it for a second and looked at the

books I'd lent Darchuk. In the books I liked, guys would jump right in at the beginning of the story with a bunch of action. Always grabbed me. Of course they'd slow down after that and let you get to know what was going on. I said as much to Mac.

"Sure, you have to do that, but this is fifteen minutes so I have to do it quick." He skimmed a *Penthouse*, nodded. "I'll start with 'Dear *Penthouse*, I want to tell you about an incredible night I had a few months ago with a sexy, twenty-five-year-old blonde I met in the bar. She's the first woman who ever deep-throated me and she taught me more in one night than all the other women I've slept with before or since.'"

"But that sounds like you weren't in charge," Ski said. He waved one of the magazines at Mac. "You've got to be in charge. All the guys are, in the good letters."

"How do you figure that showed I wasn't in charge?"

"You said 'met' instead of 'picked up', for one. Then she's teaching you? You can't do that. Have her do things to you. That sounds better and it'll make the guys pay attention."

"She did more things to me than any other woman...no, needs to be me...I did more things with her than with any other woman – "

"Or you could use 'to her'," Ski said.

"That makes it sound like she's not even there," I said.

Ski's eyebrows rose. "Quit being a woman, Ken. It just means Mac fucks her, she doesn't fuck him. And she could still be hot to trot."

"*With*," Mac said. "It'll work better with the rest."

Ski shrugged and we started working through the main part of the letter, Ski fighting Mac all the way.

"Damn it, you're three minutes in and you're still dancing with her...who cares how she plays with her hair...okay, wetting her lips is good, but can't she suck on her drink straw or something...about time they did some crotch grinding...why can't she give him a blow job in the truck on the way to her place?...yeah, that strip scene sounds good...who the hell cares how she smiles when you slide into her...she's got to say something, beg for more, tell you how good it feels, something...Please?...all right, the legs wrapped around you is good...c'mon, more fingernails on your back...about time you listened to me."

Finally we stopped, Ski and Mac wrung out and Darchuk and I just shaking our heads. Mac drained the last of the Tang from his glass and smiled, but Ski still looked pissed off. Probably just mad that Mac could tell a story that had never happened to him better than Ski who'd been there. In the final practice run, I lost track of what was real and what was Mac and us. Be surprised if it wasn't even getting hazy for Ski.

"That'll do it," Mac said.

"And if it doesn't?" Ski said.

"It will, but we've got backup if it doesn't."

"What backup?" Darchuk asked, looking at Mac and Ski suspiciously. "And why didn't you do all this today when you were working?"

"Had to walk Ski through that night half a dozen times to get all the details. And Norm was working close so we had to be careful. Made for slow going."

Norm was on Wayne's team and anything he heard was sure to get back to Wayne.

"How'd you have time for a backup plan, then?" Darchuk's eyes were narrow. I'd told him about Ski and Wayne's little dust-up and he'd just shaken his head. Trusted Ski not to say anything more about his married woman, but this looked bad.

"Take a pill," Mac said. "Ski and I did a letter with the Bertrand girls in it whenever Norm was around, and it came out pretty damn good."

"A lot more like *Penthouse* than this thing we're doing," Ski said.

"You can relax too," Mac said to Ski. He stood up. "If I'm wrong and the room is grooving to the straight bullshit, then we do the orgy with the Bertrand sisters. But I'm not wrong."

"I guess we'll know tomorrow," Ski said.

The rec car was packed when we got there after supper. Stacking chairs had been brought down from the dining cars and the tables piled outside temporarily. Seating for around forty people, with guys sitting on the shuffleboard table and standing at the back of the room bringing the number up to fifty. Almost the whole crew, except for some of the older guys. Even the Spaniard had shown up. Didn't speak English very well but his stories about Basque terrorists were scarier in a lot of ways than Tony's Mafia stories. Maybe it was because they were rawer without all the rough edges polished off them. And it probably helped that the Spaniard's stories came from what he'd really seen, not from what he'd heard.

"You've never told a story to this many people before," I said to Mac when I saw the crowd.

"Doesn't matter." His focus was on Wayne. "Only one person here, as far as I'm concerned." He was tense, but it wasn't the angry tension he had before a fight, more like the muscles bunching up on one of Ski's horses before it started galloping. Now we just had to see if what we had was enough.

"Let's get this show on the road," Bernie, our head foreman, yelled. Gradually the hubbub died down. "Until Wayne asked me to MC this thing I didn't think you guys could surprise me. Shows how wrong a guy can be." He waved a hand at the other two teams and us standing at the front of the car. "You've got three groups of perverts who figure they can tell you something about sex. We'll all be making up our minds if they succeed, but these guys," he pointed at the judges, "will pick the best. Or the worst, depending on your point of view."

"We want the dirtiest," Norm yelled.

"Yeah, we want smut!"

"Leather." "Blondes." "Brunettes." "Hooters." "Pussy."

"Okay, okay," Bernie said, holding his hands up. "We get the message. Is there anything you don't want?"

"After twenty days?" Curtis said. "Even your wife would look good now."

"Fuck you and the horse you road in on," Bernie said as the rest of us laughed.

"That's one thing we don't need. No horses," Norm said.

"Or cows." "Or sheep."

"No sheep?" Louis said. "C'mon, we want Tony to feel at home."

"Fuck-a you," Tony said, slamming his hand into the crook of his elbow, fist raised.

"Enough already." Bernie took a bowl from the end of the shuffleboard table. "Let's get this thing over with." He reached into the bowl and pulled out a strip of paper. "Nelson reading for the College Studs."

"All right, let's hear about them nice tight cheerleaders." "Yeah, do them on the desk." "Bend them over the desk." "Drive them home."

Nelson waited until the noise died down, papers in his hand. Finally he started reading. "Dear *Penthouse,* I'm writing to tell you about a toga party I went to a couple of months ago..." There went our Bertrand girls' story. Couldn't use something similar, especially since Nelson was working his way through the positions and the women, with help from Grier and the rest. Right up there with the best of the letters in *Penthouse,* but it was straight bullshit. Also, he was reading it like a letter and it showed. Guys were quiet, but not totally focused on Nelson. And Nelson let his education show through. We'd all seen the big words in other letters but they weren't right for this crowd. I knew they were sunk when Louis leaned over to me and asked in a loud whisper:

"What the hell does 'salacious commentary' mean?"

"Talking dirty, I think," I said.

"Then why the hell didn't he say so?" Louis said, to mumbled agreement from others.

Nelson stumbled as Bernie quieted Louis with a glare, but he rushed through the rest of the letter and sat down quickly.

"Okay, let's hear it for Nelson." The applause was polite and died down quickly. Bernie drew another slip of paper from the bowl. "Wayne's Wildmen."

Mac smiled as Wayne walked to the front of the crowd, hands empty. Probably happy that we'd know what the crowd wanted when it was our turn. Hadn't been able to tell for sure from the reaction to Nelson's letter.

"Well, I don't have any five-dollar words in my story," Wayne said, "but it goes something like this: "Dear *Penthouse*, I'd like to tell you about a woman I met a few years ago, before I got married. She was a substitute teacher at the high school in town, a tall blonde, with the most incredible ass you've ever seen. She looked like an angel but fucked like a mink. I met her – "

Wayne started working through the story, how he'd met the woman at a party at the principal's house, how she'd teased him when no one was looking, how he'd driven her home, how she'd invited him in... I looked at Mac and the others. Almost the same plot as our story and Wayne was hitting all the high notes. Most of the guys were leaning forward to listen and the rest were shifting in their seats or trying to casually adjust themselves. Wayne was using details too, the little ones like Mac had insisted on, the woman teasing him with flashes of her breasts as she took her bra off, taking it down almost to the nipples, then up again; her fingers digging into the sheets as he fucked her, her nipples' hard tips against his chest; the flush on her face when she came and the sensitivity of her pussy after. He hit them all. I was right there with him and had no doubt this had honest to Christ happened, and it had happened like Wayne was telling it. Even if it might have happened to Louis fifteen years ago or one of the others.

Mac's face was expressionless, but Ski was frowning. Darchuk just shook his head. We were sunk and he knew it. Too many similarities for even the best story-telling to help us win now. Our story didn't have any better a base, and the guys were going to go with the one they heard first. The Bertrand girls wouldn't even start to play. Mac'd been right about pure bullshit not being the answer.

"When spring came she had to move to her next job and the last night was even hotter than all the others, but that's another story." He stopped and the crew started hooting and cheering as he smiled at them. We went into a quick huddle.

"Give it your best shot," I told Mac. "At least we'll go down swinging."

"To hell with going down swinging," Mac said. "I'm winning this thing."

"Mac, maybe – "

"Shut up, Ski. You made your mind up yesterday." Mac pushed past us and stepped in front of the gang. Darchuk grabbed for his arm and missed. Ski looked at Darchuk and lifted his shoulders helplessly. Darchuk was paler than Ski now, his head jerking from side to side. We were jammed in, people all around us.

"Mac won't fuck you over," I whispered to him under cover of the applause, only half believing it.

"I'll kill the bastard if he does." Not angry, just a statement of fact.

Wayne turned his head and smiled at Mac. Mac nodded once in acknowledgement as the room quieted and Wayne stepped back to stand with his team.

"Okay, now we're going to hear from the Pine Valley Perverts with Mac doing the reading," Bernie said.

"Well that last one's going to be tough to beat," Mac said. "I've never had a teacher, at least not like that. I did have someone who taught me a lot though. Guess I should start this right though: Dear *Penthouse*, I'm writing to tell you about the most exciting woman I ever met and the summer we had together last year. I was working at Candle Lake last summer when I met Kris, the sweetest little sixteen-year-old, and I thought she was the hottest thing on the lake. Then I met her mother, Shannon, and Kris paled by comparison. Shannon was only thirty-six, on account of marrying young, and she'd been divorced for a couple of months. Not blonde, or tall or with huge tits, but a brunette, medium height with high, firm, apple-sized breasts and a heart-shaped face. Those were just things I noticed in passing though, because it was her eyes that grabbed me. One minute they sparkled with mischief, the next..."

I watched Darchuk while Mac drew the guys in with his voice, like the woman's eyes must've done to Darchuk. It was the kind of detail Mac couldn't make up. Darchuk had relaxed a bit when Mac said Candle Lake and divorced, instead of Sylvan Lake and married. Moving things one province over was a good start. Made Mac the likely person it happened to, and made it his story.

"...the first time was an accident. Shannon leaned over the cooler to get a beer and I got a good look down her halter top. She looked up and blushed when she saw me looking, but ten minutes later she was back to get a pop for her daughter and while she was bent over the cooler she talked to Kris for what seemed like hours. I drank in the view, the way her nipples stood out, the small area of white that her bikini usually covered. Finally she stood up, looked at me with a little smile on her face. I smiled at her and she blushed again, but then she smiled for real and I knew it was just a matter of time until I slept with her..."

The room was dead quiet again and even Darchuk was watching Mac. He kept his face fairly straight as Mac shifted into high gear, having the daughter go back to Saskatoon for a weekend, and him finding the mother sunbathing in their fenced-off backyard. Darchuk smiled a bit at this. Mac really heated things up as he described spreading suntan oil on her back, her undoing her top so he could do her whole back, rubbing oil down her sides near her breasts, then working down her back and legs and working up between her legs slowly, rubbing her through her bathing suit while she moaned into the pad on the lounger, her hands gripping the edges of it, her head arching back as Mac's finger slipped into her, then the hesitancy of their first kiss turning into a hunger. We were all with Mac as they stumbled from the hot backyard into the coolness of the house, as Mac stripped his clothes off and discovered she hadn't been with a man since her husband had left and he'd been boring in bed. I scanned the rest of the room and saw nothing but men being given exactly what they wanted, a classy Madonna who became a wild woman when handled properly. And Mac was making it believable by not making it sound easy. Ten minutes in and he still wasn't inside of her. She'd been horny, yet unsure, and he'd slowly calmed her fears and got her doing what they both wanted. Wayne had taken his time too, but he hadn't built the suspense like this. I doubt there was a guy in the room who hadn't felt the story in his crotch for the last five minutes.

Darchuk was nodding now, a slight smile on his face. I wondered how much of the story was his any more, and if even Mac knew where Darchuk's story left off and Ski or Mac or *Penthouse* began. Damned if I could tell.

"...and she climbed on top of me, moving slowly up and down, just enjoying the feeling of setting the pace for the first time in her life. I wanted her to speed up but she moaned as I dug my fingers into her hips, leaning forward to kiss me. 'Slow, lover, slow. You can have me fast later.' My legs trembled as it took every bit of my willpower not to start driving into her, but I focused on her face. Her eyes were closed and her hair swung slowly with her movements. She looked like an angel, calm and happy. I reached up and rolled her nipples with my fingers. She moaned and started to speed up."

We were back in *Penthouse* territory now, but in what Ski called the boring letters, the ones where the people made love and cared about each other and treated each other like human beings instead of a set of parts. Still, we all shared Mac's enjoyment as she went down on him, as they tried new positions, spending the weekend doing all the things she'd never done before and he'd always wanted to do.

"...she bounced up and down on me while she held onto the back of the lounger, building up her tempo until we both came. We heard her daughter's car pull into the driveway out front then, and she climbed off of me, giving me a quick kiss before slipping inside the house. I yanked on my T-shirt and shorts, finishing just as Kris came around the corner of the house. Turned out she was ready to go out, but I said I was too tired from work and too much sun. I didn't get into Kris's pants until the end of the summer, but that was fine because her mother was giving me as much sex as I could handle."

Mac stopped and smiled. The gang was leaning forward, waiting, hoping for more. Then they started applauding wildly.

"Way to go, Mac!" "Yes!" "Great story."

Wayne was shaking his head. Knew the odds were against him. Tony, Curtis, and Warren huddled in a circle, Tony's hands waving as he yapped at the other two. Warren nodded, but Curtis said something back to Tony. Curtis nodded to Bernie. Bernie held up his hands for silence.

"Okay, this was a hell of a lot more exciting than we expected," Curtis said, "and a lot harder to judge."

"Can't think when you've got a hard-on?" Grier asked.

"Very funny. I guess you know you guys came in third?" Curtis said. Nelson, Grier and the rest just sat there. No surprise there, even for them.

"The next two were a lot tougher." Curtis shot a dirty look at Grier. "It's hard to judge something when you're totally wrapped up in it. And it was right down to the wire." The crew were starting to mutter, so Curtis jumped ahead. "Second place goes to Wayne's Wildmen. The Pine Valley boys win."

"Yes!" Mac pumped his fist in the air in victory. Ski's eyes closed momentarily and his head went back as his breath exploded out of him. But I was mostly watching Darchuk. He just grinned briefly. He turned to leave, but before he could the gang was up and congratulating us. Darchuk and I just kept on saying it wasn't anything, it was Mac and Ski, really. Still it took a while to work our way through everyone, and before we did, Bernie handed Mac the money we'd won.

"So whatever happened to her?" he asked. "Whichever one of you was nailing her." Everyone quieted, waiting for the answer.

Mac grinned. "Well, whoever it was saw her a couple of times in Saskatoon before she decided she wanted to see someone closer to her own age and started going out with some businessman type down there."

"Tough break," Bernie said. Mac and Ski both nodded gravely. I bit my lip to keep from laughing. Now we were into the pure bullshit, but Ski could handle it if Mac couldn't.

Darchuk slipped out while I was shaking hands with Louis.

I found Darchuk half an hour later, leaning on the platform railing outside our bunk car. The sun was starting to go down and the air was slightly chilly. I leaned against the railing next to him and lit a smoke.

"Anybody ask where I went?" he asked.

"Nelson and some of the others were a bit curious so I told them you hadn't really been into doing the letter thing and this was the first time you'd heard it all the way through. Told them you were back in your room jerking off." I grinned. "You wouldn't be the only one, so they bought it."

"Thanks, I think."

I shrugged. We stood there a couple of minutes longer, enjoying the moment of softness the sunset gave us.

"It wasn't really like that?" I finally asked.

"What do you think?"

I nodded, and we were quiet until the sun was just a hint of orange on the horizon.

"When you were with Trish, was your heart always pounding and all you could think about was sex?"

"Sometimes," I said. "There were quiet times, too. Times we talked, or went for walks."

"Walks." He snorted. "Only time we walked was if we were going somewhere new to fuck."

"Fuck?"

"Fuck," he said. "That was one thing Ski got right. It was just sex."

Not for him though. He'd been in love. Or thought he was. I didn't know what to say to him about that. I was still working on figuring out what love was myself.

"What did happen with her?"

"Not sure. I wanted to see her more and more and she started having a harder and harder time getting time away from her husband. Or so she said. Ski told me to back off, tried to introduce me to some friends of her niece."

"Niece?"

"Sandra, that was her real name, was only twenty-seven. Kris was her sister's daughter and it was Ski going out with Kris, not me."

More of Mac's editing. Wasn't likely to get all the details from Darchuk, so I doubted I'd ever know what was real.

"She was pulling away, wasn't she?" I said.

"Yeah. Told me I was a nice kid." His hands were clenched tight on the railing. "A nice fucking kid." Each word was distinct, hard.

I didn't say anything. I'd dug up enough of his pain, and anything I said would be meaningless babble I'd picked up off TV. This wasn't Trish and I, and I didn't have anything else to compare it to.

We stood there a long time, until it was fully dark. Guys came across the platform, heading back to their rooms. Some nodded to us, others stopped and chatted briefly. I did most of the talking. Finally Ski came out of the next car. He hesitated when he saw us, his face hidden in the shadows caused by the light spilling out of the small windows of the bunk cars. Finally he handed us our share of the winnings.

"Mac's still swapping stories with Wayne and the other guys." He looked at Darchuk, whose face was unreadable in the dark. "Sorry Eric. I shouldn't have told Mac so much."

"You happy now?"

"Not like I thought I'd be. Wayne shut up, but that's not worth a friend."

Darchuk ran a hand over his face. "You told me not to sleep with her. You told me what was really happening. I owe you for that." Darchuk turned toward me. "It was hilarious really. Here Ski is all pissed off at me for sleeping with a married woman, but he can't stop himself from asking for all the details. And I was so excited by what was happening and so fucking proud of myself, that I told him every little thing. Twisted him into knots, since he wasn't getting any from Kris."

To my amazement Ski said nothing, just stood there waiting for Darchuk to take his shots. Darchuk realized this too. He sighed. "Don't ever fuck me over again like that, Ski." He held out his hand.

"Never," Ski said, grabbing Darchuk's hand tightly and giving it a quick shake. "We've got a small problem though."

"Yeah," Darchuk said, stiffening again.

"Wayne and Nelson want a rematch next month."

Darchuk's eyes widened, then he shook his head. He made a little noise that could almost have been a chuckle. Me, I didn't even try to hide it. I laughed out loud. Somebody up there had a very sick sense of humour. Ski smiled hesitantly, looking from one of us to the other, waiting for a response. Finally Darchuk clapped his hand on Ski's shoulder.

"You and Mac better get your asses in gear on our break and have one hell of a wild time," he said, "because you've used all the stories I've got. And I'm sure you don't want Mac to use his blow job from Donna story, do you?" Without waiting for an answer, he turned and walked into the bunk car.

Ski froze, looking like a deer caught in a truck's headlights. If only there was a road out of this shithole, a road home.

LITTLE
TYRANTS

MacAllister rubbed his head. Damn. Gramps had always said the clear booze was the best for you. Never mix your drinks, stick to one thing. Well, Gramps, Mac thought, you were right, but the rye, the vodka, the beer, they'd all tasted so good. And those fucking shooters. He knew better. At least he'd avoided the tequila. Then he'd really be hurting. He took another gulp of water and put the glass down with the half-dozen others on the coffee table. The aspirin and coffee still weren't working and now he had to contend with the noise.

"Mac, I wanna play!" Nicole, his girlfriend Brenda's five-year-old, stood at the end of the couch, watching him with her head cocked to one side, long blonde hair hanging half over one eye.

"So play. Who's stopping you?" Couldn't this kid do anything for herself?

"I'm bored. There's nothing to do in here."

"So go outside and play."

"It's too cold."

No kidding, Mac thought. Forty below might do the little twerp some good. Wasn't like the kid would freeze to death or anything, not the way she moved. The kid only had two speeds, flat out and asleep. No wonder she was so small and scrawny.

"So find something to do in here," Mac said. "Play a video game or something." He sat up, then leaned forward as his head spun. He picked up his pack of tobacco and started to roll a smoke.

"I've played them all. They're boring." She watched him for a second. "You're spilling."

"No shit." He licked the paper and sealed the smoke, shaking his head at its deformed shape. He put his pouch at the edge of the coffee table and swept the brown flakes into it. She was still watching him. "Damn it, kid, just find something to do and leave me alone."

"Why are you so grumpy?"

"I've got a headache, OK?"

"You drank too much last night, didn't you?"

"No, I didn't!"

"Yes you did. You smell just like Mom does when she goes out with Auntie Vickie." She smiled, obviously proud of herself. Mac looked at her for a second, eyes narrowed, then took a deep drag on his cigarette. He blew the smoke into her face.

Nicole stepped back, coughing and waving her hand in front of her face. "Mac – "

"Go find something to do. Play with your Christmas presents or use that colouring book your grandma gave you. Just leave me alone." Jesus, why hadn't Brenda taken the damn brat to her sister's? Or trained her better?

"Jeez, you're mean. You go out and get drunk and then you pick on me."

"Pick on you? Christ, kid, I let you watch cartoons for two hours this morning and played Nintendo with you. What more do you want?"

"You slept through the cartoons and you didn't try at Nintendo. It only lasted five minutes."

"Like your conception," Mac muttered.

"What?"

"Nothing." Too bad Brenda and her ex hadn't found something else to do for those five minutes. Or used a condom. He stubbed the cigarette out in the overflowing ashtray. "I said I'd play one game and I did. Now go to your room and play or go outside." He lay back on the couch and pulled the afghan up over himself.

Nicole looked at him for a second, then turned and stomped to her room. The door slammed. Little brat. What was that line Darchuk used about wanting to strangle one of his monster nephews? Oh yeah, retroactive abortion, that was it. Definitely the kid for it.

He picked up the remote and flipped through the channels, all two of them. Fucking soap operas. He rubbed his temples. Where was Brenda? She was supposed to bring more aspirin home with her. Damn, why had she said she'd cover for Pat at the bar? Wasn't her fault that Pat's car hadn't started. Stupid bitch probably forgot to plug it in. He turned the sound down on the TV and closed his eyes. With any luck he'd be able to sleep until Brenda got home.

He started to drift off, then snapped upright. Music blared out of Nicole's room. Shit. He swung himself to his feet, covered the distance in three strides, slammed the door open.

"Shut that fucking thing off!" he yelled. Nicole's eyes widened as she stepped back to the bed.

"But you told me to play..."

"Quietly. Christ, do I have to tell you everything?" He jabbed the stop button on the ghetto blaster. The room was suddenly silent, except for his ragged breathing. "You've got enough toys here you don't have to use the damn boom box." He gestured at the shelves crammed with toys and stuffed animals. "Play with a doll or something. Just make sure it's quiet."

She looked at him, then stepped away from the bed. Here it comes, he thought, her usual "You're not my dad, you can't tell me what to do." Kid didn't know how lucky she was that he wasn't her old man. He'd make her toe the line a lot better than that wimp did.

"You used the 'F' word. Mom told you not to do that. I'm telling."

Shit. Just what he needed, another fight with Brenda. He was in enough trouble over last night. "Go ahead. Run to Mommy just like a little baby." Her head came up and her eyes narrowed. Bingo.

"I'm not a baby," she said.

"Prove it. Act normal for once." And now for the bribe, he thought. "And if you behave, I'll play some more Nintendo with you."

She bit her lip. "Super Mario?"

"Sure. Super Mario. But only one game and no whining. Deal?"

"Deal." She pranced by him, heading for the TV. He grunted and stepped into the bathroom. Gramps had been right. Only three things to do with kids. Bribe 'em, banish 'em, or beat 'em. Too bad he could only use two of them. Course Brenda didn't think hitting a kid was right. She'd have a shit fit if he so much as laid a finger on her little darling. Mac shook his head. Wish Gramps had've thought that way. Not that it'd done that much harm. He'd turned out normal, hadn't he? He heard the familiar beep-beep of the game. He sighed as he flushed the toilet, then smiled. One game and he never said he'd try.

B eep, beep, beep-beep, beep-beep. Jesus, wasn't this kid ever going to finish her turn so he could die quickly and get this shit over with? Mac closed his eyes and took another drag on his cigarette, his third since the game began. Little bitch was just showing off now, rubbing his nose in it to get even for him swearing. Too bad they weren't playing something where they killed things. At least that'd make him feel a little better.

"Twenty thousand, Mac, see." She smiled quickly at him before staring at the TV again, her small fingers mashing the buttons as she bobbed and weaved with the little man on the screen.

"Yeah, I see." He hadn't even broken a thousand yet. Beep, beep, beep. God, his head. Definitely the last time he let some stacked shooter waitress talk him into another round for the boys. No aspirin, no beer for hair of the dog, what a shitty way to spend a day. Beep, beep, beep, wheee.

"Next level, Mac. Look!" She clapped her hands in delight.

"Enough!" He reached over and flipped the game off.

"Maaaac..." She turned and looked at him. She opened her mouth to speak. He inhaled deeply from his cigarette and held the smoke in, waiting. She closed her mouth and pursed her lips. Then, locking eyes with him, she wiggled backwards across the carpet out of range.

"One, two, three, four," she counted. He let the smoke out in a rush. It caught in his throat and he started coughing, a hacking cough that dug painfully into his chest. She squirmed even farther away as he bent over. Smart-ass little bitch. He pushed himself up quickly, put a hand to the floor to steady himself as his head swam.

"Kid, you're gonna pay for that." He held himself still, waiting for the spots to fade from his vision.

Nicole got to her feet and shook her head. "You're not my dad. You can't do anything to me." She turned to go to her room. "And if you try, I'll tell Mom." She walked away, back straight, head high.

"Get back here." She ignored him, closing the door after herself. He lay on the floor, waiting for his head to clear. His heart raced; his hands clenched into fists. He'd show the brat. He wasn't Brenda; he wouldn't put up with shit like that. Little monster needed to learn what it was like to have to eat supper standing up. Or to grab your ankles with your pants down while Gramps stretched out the punishment, making you tremble with fear as you waited and waited for the first blow. Brenda should've taught the little bitch stuff like that a long time ago.

Brenda. Couldn't mess that up. Best thing he'd had in a long time. Maybe ever. Good cook, great lay. Did he want to lose that?

He unclenched his fists, fought the anger. Couldn't beat on the kid like she was some asshole who'd got in his face in the bar. Good as that felt. Couldn't let her get away with defying him like that either, though. Needed to do something. He grabbed the water glass off the coffee table, took a sip, then gulped the rest down. God, what he'd do for a beer. He got to his feet slowly, looked at the door to her room, then walked to the kitchen. No orange juice left, no milk, both emptied this morning. Jesus, why didn't Brenda keep this damn place better supplied? He refilled the water glass and drank deeply. Why couldn't the kid take the bribe or the banishment?

The music started again, clear as a bell through the thin walls of the house, louder than ever. Mac slammed the glass into the sink. Glass sprayed out. He stumbled back. God damn brat.

Nicole was curled up on the bed with the ghetto blaster in her arms when he burst into the room.

"Shut that fucking thing off." He advanced on her, fists clenched again.

"No! And I'm going to tell Mom for sure now."

He stopped at the edge of the bed, glaring down at

her. "Last chance. Shut it off." His gut was tight, the adrenaline singing through his system.

She curled tighter around the ghetto blaster. "I don't have to and you can't make me."

"Little bitch." He grabbed her arm in one hand, tore it away from the ghetto blaster. He grabbed the boom box with his other hand, yanked it out of her grasp, smashed it down on her dresser. The music died abruptly.

"You were warned," he said, squeezing her arm. "You had to push though, didn't you?"

"That hurts!" she screamed, pulling helplessly against his grip. Her tears splattered his hand as he yanked her toward him. "Let me go or I'm telling Mom."

"Go right ahead. Tell her I used the 'F' word while you're at it. Fuck, fuck, fuck," he said, shoving his face within inches of hers. He pushed her back onto the bed, letting go of her arm. "Now stay in here and think about the way you acted."

He slammed the door on the way out, collapsed on the couch. Close, too close. Now he needed a story for Brenda before the kid made a big deal out of nothing. He'd jollied the old lady through problems before, he could do it again. Probably get cut off for another month now. Something else the kid was responsible for.

He almost didn't hear her door open, he was so lost in thought. A small scrape. He turned.

"I told you to stay in your room. Now get your ass back in there."

"You hurt me and I'm going to tell Mom." She was still crying, soft sobs, as she held her arm with her other hand.

"I just squeezed your arm. Don't be such a baby." He waited to see if it would work again.

"You hurt me. I'll tell Dad too."

Mac laughed. Like that little shit could do much about it. Not unless it was in an alley, from behind, with help. "Quit whining. Your mom will be home in a while and you can tell her." Plenty of time to get a story together. He started rolling a smoke.

He saw her step out of the room from the corner of his eye. Little brat was either stupider than he thought, or had a lot more balls. "Get back to your room."

"No." She took another couple of steps into the room, slowly, tremulously. Mac lit his cigarette. Kid just didn't know when to quit. Hurt. Hah. Gramps or Dad would've shown her hurt. He looked at her and stomped his foot. She took a step back, then ran past him to the kitchen. She clambered onto the chair by the phone.

"Shit!" He dropped the cigarette into the ashtray. Small fingers were punching buttons when he tugged the phone out of her hand and hung it up. "God damn it, quit it already and go to your room."

"No. You hurt me and I'm telling Mom now." She struggled to pull the phone from his grip.

The adrenaline was singing in him again, the rush he got when somebody was in his face. "Get to your room or else."

"Or else what?" Nicole's face was white beneath the tears but she kept tugging on the phone.

"You don't want to know, you little brat." The rush was in him now, his fist closing automatically. A little voice in him said take the banishment kid, but it vanished as the singing grew. His muscles tightened, he felt himself grinning.

"You hurt me – "

Something snapped. He swung, twisting at the last instant, his fist flying past Nicole's head, driving through the drywall.

They both froze. She stared at him, open mouthed. He rode out the last of the rush.

"Shut the fuck up," he said. He yanked his hand out of the wall. "Go to your room." She jumped down, ran to her room. He sank onto the chair, stared at his bleeding hand, trembled. What the hell had he done? He watched the blood ooze from the scrapes. He heard the engine whine as Brenda downshifted to turn into the yard.

OK, no problem. He'd tell her they were just playing. Shit, she'd never believe that. The car stopped, the motor dying. Fuck, the kid was gonna be making a capital case out of everything, whining about being hurt, being scared.

Scared! Yeah. He'd just been trying to scare her. That might work.

It had to.

He wrapped a dishtowel around his hand. He'd been trying to scare her and it got outta control. Yeah. The car door slammed. He looked at the hole in the wall, white plaster streaked with blood, cracks spreading outwards. He bit his lip. Shit. Snow crunched under Brenda's boots as she came up the walk. MacAllister rubbed his head.

PRINCES
IN
WAITING

"Why are we watching this crap?" Mac-Allister asks. We're three beer into the evening, our fourth night in a row, and he's becoming his usual yappy self.

"Cause I'm interested in it," Brenda snaps. She's been working in the bar long enough to know how to handle Mac's mouth.

Me, I'm watching the TV.

"And as the Queen enters her fortieth year on the throne, Prince Charles is indeed a prince-in-waiting. Impatiently waiting, some palace sources say..."

"Aw, poor Chuckles," MacAllister says. I frown at him. I can't say I feel sorry for Charles. Not with his money. I've got an idea how he feels, though. I've been waiting for the farm for ten years. So has MacAllister.

"Shut up already!" Brenda says. I stifle a smile. Brenda's got this strange fascination with the royal family that nobody can figure out. We just stay out of her way whenever they're on the news.

"And Edward the Seventh was sixty years old when he finally succeeded Queen Victoria – "

MacAllister's laughter drowns out the rest. "Damn, I sure hope the old man don't wait that long," he says.

I laugh dutifully, but Mac's got a whole different situation. His dad doesn't care about the farm as long as he gets his rent from Mac. Sure, it'd be nice if Mac owned the land, but he had control of it and the land his Gramps left him.

I wonder at the queen's thinking. Doesn't she know what waiting does to a guy? Even a rich guy? Sitting around playing with himself for twenty years'll fuck him up even worse than he already is. But what can he do? It's what he knows. Farming's what I know, and I know Dad's thoughts on retirement all too well, though the logic always escapes me. Everyone on the Prairies knows the spiel: two-dollar wheat, the grain wars, the drought, blah, blah, blah. It's not even worth talking about anymore. Everyone ends up trotting out their favourite cliché. Dad's favourite is, "Damn Europeans are screwing up my retirement plans. Just a couple of more years, son." Sure, Dad, whatever you say. Like he'd ever give up control. He's sixty-three, a lot older than any of the other guys' dads, but he's in good shape and it isn't like there's as much grunt work in farming as there used to be. He could hang around for another ten years easy. And as far as I can tell, he hasn't even given a thought to retirement. Or even slowing down. Old fucker is just like the queen that way.

"Hey, you awake?" MacAllister is looking at me, a frown on his freckled face. Obviously, I missed a question. I'm saved by the door scraping open. Radinski and Hicks have arrived.

"It's the rest of the princes-in-waiting," MacAllister says. They look confused, so he fills them in. Brenda brings another round and places it on the scarred table.

"Shit, I can just see it," Radinski says, taking his ball cap off, then settling it back on his head. "The shape the old man is in, I'll be sixty and he'll still be around doing all the chores, saying he's good for another couple of years."

We laugh, but I notice Hicks stops before the rest of us. As if he had to worry. Partner to his dad, lots of land in his name, a wife and kids, his own house. The rest of us should be so lucky.

"For sure," MacAllister says. His cheeks are flushed, usually a good sign the beer is hitting him. I've seen it a lot in the last couple of months. Just like I've seen the inside of this damn bar, the ratty puke brown carpet, the big-titted women in the beer posters, the beat-up pool table. Jesus, I don't even know my trailer this well.

"Should start our own club," MacAllister is saying. "Secret handshakes and all that shit."

"And in every town," Ski says. I shake my head. Wish I could take things that lightly. Ski's got me thinking, though, and I can't get the picture out of my mind. Sixty. Grey haired. Fat. Wrinkled. Sitting alone in an old dump of a trailer. Still waiting. Lovely thought. Time to change the subject.

"Heard from Darchuk lately?" I ask Ski. He frowns.

"Yeah, talked to him on the phone the other night. He got back from Florida last week. Said you wouldn't believe the babes down there."

"What's a babe?" MacAllister asks, a puzzled look on his face. We laugh. The joke is old, but if we don't laugh we'll cry. We all know there are only two types of women in town: high school girls and married women. Trouble either way. Every other woman gets the hell out as soon as she graduates from high school. Who can blame them? It's not like there's anything out here for them. I gulp down half a beer. Getting really depressing tonight, I tell myself. I told myself I wasn't going to do this anymore.

"Circle the wagons," I say to Brenda. It's Saturday night, got a couple of weeks before seeding, I'm with my buddies, we've got the bar to ourselves and the beer is cold and good. Who needs to be depressed? I say, "You see that fight on TV the other night," and we're off. No more of that serious shit. The beers flow by and we talk of the hockey playoffs, the Blue Jays' chances this year, cars, women, hunting, and government incompetence. The talk keeps the picture of the lonely old man away and I relax into the groove, hoping it will last. I should know better by now.

"You see that article in the *Western Producer* about zero till?" Ski says. Damn. Would one night without this farm shit be too much to ask?

"Yeah," Hicks says. "A lot of good stuff in there. That list of all the nutrients that you keep in the land when you don't work the shit out of it was great. Might get some of these old farts to finally get the hint and quit burning their straw." He stops, looks at me and winces when he realizes what he's said. I look at him for a second, take a long pull from my beer.

"That would require the old farts to have a clue," I say. Or listen to their sons. I can still see the flames behind the old man as we argued. His land, his rules. Ignorant old prick. "Mostly they just want to do things like they've done them from day one."

"No doubt," Ski says. "It's like pulling teeth to get the old man to do anything."

"At least he'll listen," I say. I look at Mac. His face is tight and he's glaring down at the table. Time to change the subject. I open my mouth to speak, but Hicks butts in.

"You've got to make them listen. Christ, do they think things are going to get better? Prices sure the fuck aren't going to improve and you can't depend on the government. The only thing to do is cut costs."

I grab my beer as Mac slams his fist down hard on the table.

"You fucker. Cut costs. Well, Daddy's little boy, where the fuck should we cut? The extras?" He stretches his legs out so we can see the scuffed leather of his cowboy boots, the soles almost worn through. "Maybe I can get by without clothes?" He starts to stand. Ski puts his hand on Mac's arm.

"Relax, Mac."

"Relax? That little – "

"Shut up, Mac. We're here to have fun, not fight."

"Fun?" Mac says as he pushes himself away from the table. "Fun, my ass!" He pulls his arm out of Ski's grip, turns and stumbles to the bathroom. We're silent as he slams the door behind him. I look at Ski and shrug.

"What's biting his ass?" Hicks asks. He looks shaken.

I look at him, at the leather jacket and three-hundred-dollar boots, and shake my head. "You mean you didn't know about him losing the lease on that government pasture?"

"No, no I didn't. I've been busy getting my equipment ready for seeding. Haven't seen much of anybody lately."

"Yeah, well he did, so let's just lay off the farming talk for a while." I hear another slam from the can. I bite my lip and meet Ski's look. I shrug. Sounds like Mac's having a sit down. Question is, is he cooling off or working himself up for round two? Getting so none of us can read him.

"Well, looks like we've got a few minutes before Mac's back," Ski says dryly. He pushes his hat back on his head and looks at me. "Hicks is right, you know. You've got to start getting into zero till. It's going to be the only way to farm in ten years."

"Jesus, you're as bad as him," I say, waving toward Hicks. Surprised he hasn't said anything. Guess pissing off one person a night is enough for him. "They don't give the chemicals away. And the equipment sure the fuck ain't free." I lean forward. "Or maybe you figure I should cut costs too?"

Ski frowns. "No, we're all to the bone right now. You just start small. One field at a time. That's how I'm doing it. Rent or borrow the equipment. Shit, what you save in the first year in fuel will cover the chemicals. And you've got to fertilize anyway."

"And where am I supposed to get the money up front. The Credit Union? That'd give them a good laugh." Overextended, that prick of a manager had said. Poor credit risk. And would the old man co-sign so I could get the loan? Why waste money on a fad, he'd said. A fad. Thanks for the support, Dad. It's nice to know how much you value my opinion, how equal partners we are. Must be about how Charles feels. All you get to do is wait. You don't get any control. The picture comes back to me. An old fat man. Waiting.

"So you'd sooner sit and watch your topsoil blow away whenever there's a big wind?" Ski asks.

"I don't have cousins to borrow equipment from," I say as sarcastically as I can. "Some of us have to do things on our own."

"I pay for anything I get," he snaps. "The old man hasn't helped me on this."

"Yeah, right."

He lifts his hat and resettles it on his head. "Maybe if you didn't spend all your time in here you might have some money. You're – " He stops as we hear the door slam in the can. "Later," he says, then jumps into a story about his Trans-Am. Later? What the fuck does that mean? I watch Mac come out of the can. Seems calm enough, not that that means anything with Mac. He drops into his chair, picks up his beer, takes a drink. I look at him. He looks back, his face blank. Damn. I feel my heart beat faster.

"That car hit eighty by the time I was at Bayne's corner," Radinski says. "Gravel spraying everywhere, the whole damn thing shaking. I thought Darchuk was going to shit."

"Darchuk," MacAllister says. His face is flushed deep red from the beer. I look at Ski. We both know the mood. Just what we need, over six feet of pissed-off scrapper. "Fucking lucky bastard," MacAllister continues. "Shagging the bimbos in Florida." He looks at me. "Hey. Weren't you supposed to go with him?"

"Yeah, but the engine went on the tractor, remember?" As if he didn't know that.

"Oh yeah. Got it fixed yet? Been two months. Only got a couple of weeks before seeding."

"I'm getting there." I try to keep calm. Mac was always good at knowing what scabs to pick at. I don't want to think about that fucking tractor and he knows it.

"Christ, man, you forget how to use a wrench?"

"Fuck off, MacAllister." My fists are clenched under the table. He frowns, then shrugs.

"Just asking. Don't be so damn touchy."

"Yeah, fine. Let's just drop it," I say. "Okay?" A whole winter of grabbing whatever work I could find, busting my butt for the trip, then bye bye money. Same old song and dance. The farm always came first. I unclench my fists. Wouldn't solve anything anyway.

"Hey, Hicks, how come your old lady let you come out to play tonight?" Ski puts his hand on Hicks' arm.

"For Chrissake, Mac, quit being a dickhead," he says. Out of the corner of my eye I see Brenda moving and wave at her to stay put. Mac and her had something going a couple of years ago and the split hadn't been friendly. She'd just set him off.

"Hey, I ask a few questions and I get shit on." Mac

glares at Ski, who watches him silently. No reaction, no fear. Even drunk, Mac knows better. "Can't shithead talk for himself?"

"Yes, asshole, I can." Hicks lurches out of his chair knocking it over. The beer splashes out of his glass as he bumps the table. Oh shit.

"Okay, then tell me something," MacAllister says, standing up himself to tower over Hicks. "Does your wife still give good blow jobs? Best I ever had."

"Bastard!" Hicks lunges. Before I realize what I'm doing, I'm out of my chair wrestling him back. I hear Brenda yelling and MacAllister swearing. I get a good grip on Hicks and risk a look. Ski has MacAllister pinned against the wall, though he isn't trying to get loose. Good. Ski's bigger than Mac, but five years ago it would've taken three of us to do that. Ski is talking quietly, but all I hear is Hicks' deep breathing.

"You okay now?" I ask him.

"That motherfucker – "

"Relax. He's just had too much to drink. He doesn't know what he's talking about."

"Bastard says another thing about my wife, I'll kill him."

"Yeah, I know." I let go of him but stay between him and MacAllister. "Let it go for now. Talk about it when you're sober." Not that they would, but it'll cool things off for now. "You came with Ski, right?" He nods. "Then I'll drive you home."

"But..." He looks at MacAllister. Doesn't want to look like he's running away.

"It's okay. He's out of here too."

Hicks hesitates, then Brenda looks at him. She mouths the word "please."

Hicks nods. We pick up our jackets and head for the door.

"Leaving, asshole?" MacAllister says.

"Shut up, Mac," Brenda says. "Please, Hicks, just go."

"Yeah, just go," MacAllister mimics. Hicks stiffens, but I push him through the doorway and slam the door behind us. We're silent as we walk to the car.

"Beer," I say and reach into the back. I fish two out of yesterday's case and hand one to Hicks. He's silent as we open them and take a deep drink. The only sound is the Mustang's starter dragging. The beast is showing its age. I head us out of town.

"He didn't mean what he said," I say. "Shit, he was just looking for a reaction."

"A fight you mean."

"That too." I shred the label on my beer with my thumbnail. I drain half of it. "Look, Mac's had some troubles – "

"We've all got fucking troubles. That's no excuse for what he said."

"No, but..." Hicks is right, but I want him to see MacAllister's frustration. How can I get him to understand, though? "Look, Mac's hurting right now. There's the land, and then no work – "

"Maybe if he didn't always get in fights and tell the boss to fuck off, he could get a job."

"Yeah, but... Look, he's a good worker. Sitting on his ass bugs him."

"Doesn't seem to mind sitting in the bar."

I bite back my reply. Fuck this. Waste of my time. "You know Mac. Too much booze, he gets stupid."

"Then why does he drink?" Hicks asks. I shrug, draining my beer. Why do any of us? I turn into his driveway. He finishes his beer and hands me the bottle.

"Thanks for the ride." He gets out and slams the door. I watch him walk over the neatly trimmed lawn, past the swing set to the big split-level. He goes inside and I shake my head. Daddy's little boy. I put the bottle away, then look around the yard. Big barn, big new equipment, the whole nine yards. Shit, some of my equipment is older than I am. I look at the zero tillage equipment neatly lined up by the shop and sigh. I've got about as much of a chance of getting all Hicks has as I do of inheriting Buckingham Palace. I shake my head. Starting to lose it. I back the Mustang out, hoping Mac will be gone when I get back. I open another beer.

I get lucky. Radinski's truck is gone when I pull up in front of the bar. Brenda is washing glasses when I walk in.

"Still open?" I ask.

She shrugs. "Why not? Beer?"

"Make it a double rye and coke. And get yourself one." I sit and watch her pour the drinks with quick, jerky movements.

"Ski said to wait," she says. "He'll be back as soon as he settles Mac down." She sits, handing me my drink. I gulp it and wish I hadn't relaxed on the drive in, wish I hadn't had time to remember that damn picture of the lonely old man waiting. The warmth of the rye flows down my throat. Two more gulps and it's gone. Brenda sips her drink and points at the bar. I get up and pour another one.

"Could be hours before Mac settles down," I say.

"Maybe." She frowns as I push the glass under the dispenser a second time. "Little heavy isn't that?"

"I'm too old for this shit," I say.

"That's tonight. What about the last couple of months."

"I don't want a fucking lecture." I try a smile. It's weak but it's the best I can do. "Can we just change the subject?"

"Like every other time?" she says. "I give up." We sip our drinks silently for a minute before she says, "You know, I saw another documentary on Charles last week. They talked about his role as Prince of Wales and all the good he's done on the land he got with the title. I guess he's really careful with his own land."

"What the hell is that supposed to mean?" I glare at her. She just smiles softly as she looks into her drink.

"Not a damn thing." Her smile widens. "It was kind of neat though, seeing Charles driving a tractor around all dressed up in his tweeds." She chuckles, then frowns when I don't laugh too. She shrugs. "Look, it's your life, your choice, but I think you're making a mistake. You're carrying this poor-misunderstood-farmboy-who-don't-get-no-respect crap too far." With that she swings into a story about her daughter's piano lessons. I try to listen but can't keep track. Have I been that bad?

That obvious? I still don't have an answer when Ski walks in half an hour later.

I clench the handrail tightly as I try to get down the bar's outside steps without stumbling. Radinski's ahead of me with a case of beer. He flings it onto the seat in his truck, then turns to look at me.

"I'll drive," he says. I want to argue, but I find myself swaying. He's right, so I get in.

"Your place, my place, or cruising?" he asks.

"Home," I say, opening a beer. "Gotta work on the tractor tomorrow." He looks at me and raises an eyebrow.

"I do," I say, but I don't even sound convincing to myself. He shrugs and starts the truck.

"How about a little cruise," he says. "I see enough of my place during the week."

"Home," I say. Out of the corner of my eye I see him look at me. I keep staring out the windshield. He shakes his head.

"Christ, I don't know which is worse, MacAllister flipping out or you sulking."

"I'm not sulking."

"Right." He opens a beer for himself. "At least I know where I stand with Mac."

"Mind your own business."

"Fine." He drives silently for a minute. He pulls his cap off and resettles it. "You know, Mac talked on the way home. A lot of it didn't make much sense, but he talked."

"I don't wanna talk and I don't need you playing shrink."

"Jesus H. fucking Christ!" I grab the dash as he slams on the brakes. Beer splashes out of my bottle. He rams the gearshift into park and swings to face me.

"It was one fucking trip!" he says. "Get over it already. You can't brood forever."

"It's not the fucking trip," I say. Son of a bitch thinks he knows me.

"Then what? You haven't done bugger all for the last two months but sit around and whine. Fuck, quit looking at the shitty side of things and do something for once. Your tractor – "

"Fuck the tractor," I say. "This isn't about the trip, it isn't about the tractor and it isn't about the zero till." And I mean it. They just got me thinking. Thirty years old and trying to make a living with three quarters of not-so-great land and fifty cows and no hope for any more in the near future. I tried telling myself that I liked being a farmer. It was true, but it didn't work. Nor did thinking about the pleasure of owning my own land. Not when the bank owned more than I did. Shit, I barely owned the fenceline.

"What is it then?" Ski asks. I shrug. It's none of his business. I'll take care of things on my own. Somehow, some way, I'll get the old man to see things my way. Probably about the time Charles gets the throne.

"Look, if it's about that zero till crap," Ski says, "we can work something out. I'll talk to Hicks and my cousins, see about working some sort of rent thing out."

"I told you I don't have the money."

"So work it back. Fuck, you want me to do all your thinking for you?"

"No, I want you to mind your own fucking business."

"Fine," he says, and starts the truck moving. "Brood away then. I tried." I want to say something, to tell him I appreciate the concern, but nothing comes out. We drive in silence until we reach my place. The old man plays on my mind. Two more years. Two more years. No respect. No control.

"Thanks for the ride," I say, opening the door as Ski stops in front of the trailer.

"Yeah. See you." He looks at me. "Call if you need a hand with the tractor."

"Sure." I get out, close the door and watch him drive away.

The trailer is dark. I stumble in, heading for the fridge. I grab a beer, take a sip. Doesn't taste as good as before. I wander into the living room, shovel the clothes off the couch so I can sit down, and look out the picture window. There's enough of a moon that I can see the coffee table in front of it. My graduation picture is just a shape, but I've got it memorized anyway. All us kids, tuxes, and too much hair, gowns, and acne. Now there were an engineer, a couple of teachers, businessmen, and a geologist in that small group. Of course, there were also farmers, housewives, and labourers. And a borderline drunk. "Our great and unlimited future," Darchuk had said. Uh-huh.

I look out the window. A barn, a garage, some granaries, and my land. Not enough of a farm of course, not now, not in this economy, but mine anyway. It should be enough, has been enough, but the picture keeps on playing. An old fat man waiting. Waiting. Then another picture, Brenda's picture. Charles bouncing across a field on a tractor, tweed jacket, elbow patches, the whole nine yards. I chuckle, then look out again. The garage. My tractor. I nod, sip the beer, then put it down. I reach for the phone and pull it over to me, then curl up on the couch. I'm so fucking tired. The tractor. Tomorrow. My eyes close. I'll call Ski. Tomorrow...

ALL THE
CRAZY HORSES

Radinski woke slowly, bladder screaming, mouth dry. The woman was a dead weight on his arm, her skin slick with sweat against him. The bedroom was hot, confining. He slowly slid his arm from under her, careful not to wake her. She moaned and he froze, free only to his elbow. Her back was to him, her long tangled mane of brown hair across his arm. Inch by inch he worked his arm out until his hand was free. For once he was on the outside of the bed so he didn't have to slide off the end. Now he just eased himself off the side, careful not to let the springs creak. He stood and looked down at her.

She'd pushed the blanket down to her waist, the curve of her butt starting an inch or so before the blanket, the tan line just visible. He looked at the swell of her hips, the sheen of sweat, and smiled. He could see the curve of the side of her breast. He remembered how they'd looked, large, firm, superb. He felt himself hardening. Time for a morning glory? He bit his lip, remembered the night before. The sex had been good, considering how much they'd both had to drink, but it wasn't like it had been a real wild ride or anything. Straight missionary position, not even her legs wrapped tight around him, though she had been spurring him on with her nails. He was too tired for the drawn-out escape that would follow, though, the breakfast full of strained silences, awkward laughter, the obligatory phone number. Call me. Yeah, right. You both knew better, so why bullshit each other? Better this way, clean and quick.

He scooped his clothes up, making as little noise as possible. Bathroom was only a couple of steps from the bedroom, if he remembered right. Quick piss, dress in there, then away he went. Truck was down the block so she wouldn't even hear him leave. He eased the door open, backed out, his clothes bundled in front of him, and then quietly closed the door.

He jumped as somebody gasped behind him. He twisted around. Ten feet away a pair of kids sat on the couch, frozen at the sight of him. The woman's face looked back at Ski in miniature. A colouring book lay open on the floor where the girl must have dropped it. A boy sat by her, a book on his chest, eyes wide.

Shit.

He pulled the clothes tight to his crotch, crabwalked sideways toward the open door, their eyes following him as he stumbled backwards into the bathroom. He slammed the door behind him. The wood was cool on his ass as he leaned against it. He tried to think as he heard the kids argue.

"Ryan, what – " The girl's voice was high, thin. Ski heard the fear, the uncertainty, just like the time him and his brother were arguing during a drunk and his niece, Candace, came out of her bedroom, crying and trembling, scared of the yelling, the situation she didn't understand.

"Just be quiet, Stephanie." The boy's voice was sharp and Ski could hear the edge of panic he was trying to hide.

"But – "

"Just be quiet. Please." Ryan's voice softened. "I'll explain later."

"But – " Ski heard the catch in the girl's voice as she tried not to cry.

"Please!"

He waited for her reply. Silence. He listened carefully. Quiet sobbing. Shit, shit, shit. What kind of stupid broad boffed somebody when her kids were in the house? And she'd left claw marks on his back for them to see. Damn. Or maybe he'd been lucky and the kids couldn't see them. There had to be a good side to hair on the back, didn't there?

He shook his head. At least he hadn't gone for the morning glory. It would've been an even bigger mess then. He dropped his clothes, flipped on the switch for the fan, stepped up to the toilet. The splashing in the bowl drowned out the murmur of the kids' voices. He finished, flushed, splashed water on his face. Now what? Make enough noise to wake up Terri or Mary or whatever her name was? Terri, that was it. He pulled his clothes on, straining the bits and pieces of last night through the sieve he called a memory. She was proud of her daughter. Pictures, the whole bit. The kid reminded him of his niece, Candace, in more ways than one, same age, same hair colour, even a bit of a resemblance. But the kid was supposed to be at Terri's sister's. Fuck, she'd lied to him. Ski buttoned his shirt. No, she'd been reluctant to come home, but they were both too ready, the farm too far to drive to. He'd talked her into it.

He pulled the medicine cabinet open. No aspirin. Damn. He swung the door shut and looked at himself. Hair sticking up all over the place, thick stubble, eyes red, lips puffy. Definitely not the "sort of Tom Selleck look" that Terri had bullshitted him with in the bar. He smoothed his moustache down. He was surprised the kids hadn't screamed. God knows he wanted to. How'd he get into this? And how was he going to get out of it? He rubbed his temples. There was something scratching around the edges of his memory, something from the warm fuzzy time after sex while they were both drifting off to sleep.

Later. He stuffed his socks in his pockets, not trusting his balance enough to pull them on, afraid he wouldn't want to get up if he sat down. What to do? Waking her up was a bad idea. It'd be a fucking soap opera. He looked at the small window, stifled a smirk. Little bit late in the slutting career to be crawling out a window. Besides, that was supposed to be from an angry husband, not a couple of kids. It was too small for him to fit through anyway.

He ran his fingers through his hair, trying to smooth it down. Jesus, Ski, he thought, the terror of every bar across northern Saskatchewan scared of a couple of kids?

Fucking terrified.

He put his hand on the knob, took a deep breath. Quick and easy, same as before. Get his boots at the door and get out. He pulled the door open.

The kids were both on the couch now, the little girl curled up next to the boy, wiping her nose with a kleenex. The boy fixed him with a glare, his eye gleaming through his glasses.

"Hi." Ski's voice was strained, hoarse from too much whisky, too many cigarettes. He started across the room, feet sliding on the hardwood floor, long strides pulling him towards the door.

"Who are you? What were you doing in my mommy's bedroom? Why isn't she awake?" The girl's words were like a leash, yanking him to a stop. Ski looked at her. She was curled tight to the boy's side, knees pulled up, arms clenched tight to her chest. Her cheeks were wet, eyes wide. The boy had his arms around her, holding her tight, a ten-year-old body-guard. He cut Ski off before he could speak.

"She's just still sleeping, Stephie." The boy looked up and met Ski's eyes. "Why don't you just go?"

"Uh, okay. Sure." Anything to avoid explaining what he'd been doing in her mom's room. He stepped toward the door but a quiet sob stopped him again. He turned, looked into the girl's frightened eyes. Shit. This wasn't what he wanted. His brother always laughed at the way his nieces wrapped him around their little finger, how all it would take was a sniffle to break him down. Ski had told him over and over that he was full of it, but now he wondered. He stepped back to the coffee table, dropped to one knee, met her eyes.

"It's okay, Stephanie. Or should I call you Stephie?" She stopped sobbing, sniffled, stayed silent. "Anyway, my name is Ski." He stopped, tried to think of something believable, something she might understand, something that wouldn't scare her worse. She was like a skittish colt and he had to quiet her down by talking. Slow and calm, that was the way. Then when she was calm he'd lead her where he wanted her to go. Kind of like with a woman. "Look, your mom is okay. She's – "

"Then why isn't she awake? She's always awake when I get home from Aunt Sherry's."

Aunt. The other kid must be her cousin. Then the last piece falls into place. He remembered her arm stretched across his chest, the click as she turned the alarm on. "It's been great, but you've got to be gone in the morning," she'd said. Fine, he'd thought, he wouldn't have to go through all the fake emotional stuff. A clean quick exit. At her request, yet. He'd lain there half asleep, smiling as her breathing slowed, became regular. Then he'd looked at the clock. 4:30. The alarm was set for seven. No way. He'd reached out, snapped it off.

Oh shit. He'd fucked up big time. Again. Bad enough he'd terrified his own niece with drunken stupidity, he shouldn't do it to some kid he didn't even know. He licked his lips, tried to figure a way out of the mess he'd help create. Had to make it good. Kids didn't need to know this kind of stuff.

"Your mom, she was up late last night. And I don't

think her alarm went off." And it was only 8:30. And she'd had a shitload to drink.

"Why was she up late? What was she doing? Why didn't you have any clothes on?"

"Uh, she was, that is, we were, uh – "

"She was celebrating Kathy's birthday," the boy said quickly. Ski thanked him with a quick nod.

"So why didn't you have any clothes on?"

Oh shit. He'd hoped she wouldn't get back to that question. He looked at the boy but he wasn't giving Ski any help on this one. Looked to be enjoying his discomfort even. What to say? Couldn't say "Because your mom was giving me a wild ride." Wasn't really true anyway. He ran a hand over his sweaty face. Had to tell her something.

"It's really hot in here," he said, "and I get a rash from my clothes when it's hot."

The boy closed his eyes and grimaced. Ski knew how he felt.

"Is that why your back has all those red scratches on it?" she asked.

It was Ski's turn to grimace. The boy looked at the ceiling, his lower lip caught between his teeth. "Yeah, the heat's what causes that." God, that was even lamer than the lines he'd used on women when he was a teenager. He just hoped she was as gullible as some of the girls back then.

"That doesn't sound right. You're lying. What – "

The boy finally took pity on Ski. "Stephie, he answered your question. And I've got a friend who gets rashes like that."

"Really? Sounds pretty dumb to me."

"Really," the boy said. Ski found himself holding his breath. Believe him, he thought. He was too tired and hungover to think of anything that wasn't just as stupid.

"Well, okay, but I still want to know what he's doing here."

That one was easier. "I was the designated driver so I had to drive your mom home when she had too much to drink." Ski smiled at her, hoping, praying, that the sniffling would stop. Her mom had shown him pictures. She was cute when she wasn't crying. He'd even been able to be honest when he saw the pictures. No "mmm, yeah, cute kid" said with a serious look on his face. Her mom had been proud of the kid. And she hadn't wanted to bitch about her ex. Ski had liked that. An evening of "Yeah? What an asshole," got boring real quick.

"Why – " the girl started before the boy interrupted again.

"Stephie, he can't stay here all day answering your dumb questions. He's probably got somewhere to go."

Ski took the hint, stood up to leave. Kid knew way too much for his years. And he'd saved Ski's ass big time. "Yeah, I do. Got bales to haul today."

"You're a farmer?" the girl asked.

"Yeah, about forty minutes out of town." Another chunk of memory surfaced. "Your mom told me you like horses. Me too. Got a couple of quarter horses you'd love." She stayed curled up against her cousin, eyes intent on Ski. The sniffles had stopped, but she was still tight with fear. He'd talked her down a bit but now he had to lead her away from where she shouldn't be. He stepped back to the edge of the coffee table, crouched. He had to brace himself against it. He smiled at her and pointed at the half-coloured brown horse in the colouring book. "That looks like Pokey, my first pony, the one I had when I was Ryan's age. He was a real little butterball. Loved to take sugar right out of my hand."

"What happened to him?" Her arms uncrossed and her hands dropped to her sides. She leaned slightly forward.

"He got old and we put him out to pasture. Now I've got a horse called Mad Max. He runs like the wind." And was so crazy it was almost impossible to stop him. Every ride was a wild ride with that knothead.

"Did Pokey run like the wind?" she asked.

The boy snorted. "Don't be stupid. They wouldn't have called him Pokey if he did." He'd let go of the girl now and slid a little ways away. His eyes were no longer locked on Ski. Easy now. Just keep talking.

"It's not stupid. Pokey could run if he wanted to. Him and the dog would chase each other up and down the pasture for hours." Ski clip-clopped his fingers up and down the table to demonstrate. "It was just when somebody was riding him that he didn't want to run. He'd walk all day, but as soon as you kicked him to make him run he'd head for the nearest fence to rub you off. Or," Ski smiled, "he'd head for the trees, then wham," he smacked himself on the forehead, rocked back to steady himself on one hand, "he'd run you into a nice thick branch and, poof, into the dirt you'd go."

The girl giggled and even the boy smiled. Ski felt a weight lift. She wasn't scared anymore. He could leave.

He started to stand, then grabbed the edge of the coffee table as his head swam. The head smack had been a bad idea. Ski closed his eyes and took deep breaths as his head throbbed.

"Are you okay, Mr. Ski?"

"Ski, just plain Ski." He opened his eyes, blinked a couple of times to focus. He smiled at her. "Guess I took too many hits on the head from old Pokey. Got a headache now."

"Ryan can get you an aspirin, can't you Ryan."

The boy looked at her and shrugged. "Sure." He got up and headed for the bathroom. Ski let him go, not wanting to admit that he was rooting through the medicine cabinet. Ryan was back in a couple of seconds.

"Sorry. Aunt Terri's all out."

"That's okay." Ski stood up, face tight. He'd stop at the first convenience store he found and get some. And a big coffee. He walked to the door and dug his boots out of the closet. "Nice meeting you kids." He shook his head. Fucking whisky.

"Just a second, Mr. Ski." The girl got up and ran past him into the kitchen. Ski leaned against the door, boots in hand as she climbed on a chair and pulled a cupboard door open. She grabbed a bottle and jumped off the chair. "Mommy always gives me these when I don't feel good." She handed him a bottle of children's Tylenol.

"Stephie – " Ryan started.

"Shh," Ski said, waving a hand at the boy. He slid slowly down the wall until he knelt eye to eye with her. He took the bottle from her hand as she struggled to open it. "Thanks, Stephie." He was surprised at the warmth he felt, like when one of his nieces gave him a hug for no particular reason. The lid popped off and he shook a couple of tablets onto his palm, popped them into his mouth. He crunched them with his teeth. Grape flavoured. Kind of tasty actually. He smiled at her again and she giggled.

"Your teeth are purple." She put her hand to her mouth to stop the laughter. Ski chuckled, rubbed his finger over his teeth and looked at it.

"Yep, purple all right." Even Ryan laughed.

Ski stood, ruffled the little girl's hair. "Thanks, Stephie. That helps a lot. I've got to be going though." His stomach grumbled, craving food, the greasier the better. Aspirin, McDonald's, coffee and a large Pepsi. Something clicked. He looked around the room, then into the kitchen. No dishes in either room.

"Have you two ate?"

"We had a bit of toast at Aunt Sherry's, but Mom usually cooks us a big breakfast." They'd be lucky if she woke up by noon, he thought. Of course, they could always have cereal. Or wake Terri up. Leave, he told himself.

Stephie was looking at him, the tears wiped from her face. Ryan also looked at him, no longer tight and angry, but watchful. The room was warm and homey, with a homemade rug over the hardwood floor, family pictures on the wall and Stephie's picture books mixed with her mom's novels on the coffee table. Ski thought of his house, the mess waiting for the next time his brother brought the wife and kids over and guilt drove Ski to clean, the television playing all day to provide company. He looked at his watch. What the hell, the bales weren't going anywhere.

"What kind of breakfast? Eggs and pancakes I bet."

"Yeah, sometimes."

"Well, I can do better. I make the best omelette you've ever had."

"Really?"

"Really!" He put his boots down and stood. "You'll have to help me though."

"I'm not s'posed to go into the cupboards," she said, scuffing her foot along the floor and looking at her mother's bedroom door.

"So point and I'll go into the cupboards. But you gotta show me where the coffee is first." Ski looked at Ryan. "You in?"

He shrugged. "Sure, why not?" He got up, walked over to Ski. "Can we have pancakes too?"

"Sure, why not?" Ski smiled. This ought to be interesting.

An hour later he was sitting at the kitchen table telling the kids yet another crazy horse story.

"Now Lady, she was a sneaky one. She wouldn't buck you off. Instead she'd puff up her chest when you were tightening up the cinch. If you didn't watch you'd end up lying in the dirt when you tried to get on her." He stopped and smiled. "At least she didn't step on you when you were down. She'd just stand there with the saddle hanging under her belly and snort at you like you were the stupidest person she'd ever seen. One time I'd swear she even shook her head at me in disgust."

Stephanie and Ryan laughed.

"Did you ever have a normal horse?" Ryan asked.

"What's normal?" Ski said. "Horses are like people; the fun ones are the ones that don't behave."

Stephie's brow wrinkled, then her face brightened as she looked behind Ski.

"Mom, you're up. Mr. Ski was just telling us about all his horses."

"I heard," Terri said. She was wearing grey sweats, her hair pulled back, traces of last night's makeup still visible. She looked good, Ski thought, as he met her guarded gaze. Neither of them looked away. Finally she nodded.

"You like his stories?" she asked Stephanie.

"Yeah. They're funny." She waved at the remains of the pancakes and half-eaten omelettes. "And he made us breakfast."

"Looks like he made enough to feed half a dozen truckers," Terri said. She sat and poured a cup of coffee. She looked at Ski and he tried to read her face. Did she want him to leave? Did she feel as strange as he did? The silence stretched on until Stephanie started to wriggle in her chair. Finally Terri's face relaxed.

"So, Mr. Ski, tell me another story," she said.

HERE BE
MONSTERS

Even though it was still before lunch, the mall was crowded with Christmas shoppers wandering like zombies from store to store, their purchases clutched tightly to their chests or swinging from their hands in brightly coloured shopping bags. Radinski leaned by the entrance of the third ladies wear store they'd been to, waiting for his girlfriend Terri to find "the perfect sweater" for her sister and watching their shopping cart. Ski shook his head. He'd liked a couple in the first store they'd been in, but no, they hadn't been quite right. Christ, it wasn't like Tanya was some sort of supermodel. She dressed okay, but Ski had never seen her in anything outstanding. He sighed. At least this was the last gift Terri had to buy. They could get out of this bloody mall soon and away from all these people.

Or not. Ski turned his head to look at a woman he'd noticed out of the corner of his eye. Nice. Very nice. She was a tall brunette wearing an oversize white sweater and black tights. Ski smiled and turned his head farther to follow the woman as she disappeared into the crowd. Almost made being in the mall worthwhile.

"Just can't help yourself, can you?" Terri said from behind him.

Oh shit. Ski twisted his head back, met Terri's blazing eyes.

"Jesus, here I think just because you say you'll change, you actually will." She grabbed the handle of the shopping cart and stomped away from Ski. He stood for a second, unsure, then went after her, his long strides quickly closing the distance between them.

"Christ, don't get so bent out of shape," he said when he caught up to her. "It was just a harmless little look."

"Like the hundred other harmless little looks I've seen you take since we started going out? Always looking for greener pastures aren't you?"

"Don't be so ridiculous. I just looked at her. Wasn't like I tried to pick her up."

"But I bet you wondered how she'd be in bed. And if she'd be better than me." Her voice was rising, making Ski glad that they'd reached the mall doors. He jumped ahead of Terri and yanked the door open. She stormed by him without the slightest acknowledgment. He hoped it wasn't a sign the silent treatment was coming.

"Terri, wait..." He rushed to catch up with her. "Why don't we go to your place and we can talk about this."

"What makes you think I want to talk about this?" she snapped.

"Because usually you never shut up," Ski snapped back as he unlocked his truck. "It's always talk about this, talk about that, with you. You figure that talking is the answer to everything."

"Maybe it would be if I had a boyfriend who ever listened." Terri heaped her bags onto the seat of the four-by-four between them, then climbed in.

"Don't be piling all this on me again. It's not like you never look. You think I don't hear when you and Tanya go on and on about Mel Gibson's butt? Or I don't know all the stories about when you went to the male strippers?"

"That's different. Those were special occasions or movie stars, not some woman from around here. Who knows, maybe you fucked her before you met me."

"Up yours. Why do you always act like I've nailed every woman within a hundred miles? It's not like I was your first."

"But you weren't my fiftieth. Christ, Ski, if you were a woman you'd be the biggest slut around. And I'm supposed to trust you?"

"If you weren't so paranoid you would. I'm not your ex-husband. I don't cheat. Christ, how many times do you have to be told that before you believe it?" He pulled up in front of the duplex that Terri shared with her daughter, Stephanie.

"Show me; don't tell me." Terri yanked the door open and jumped out. "No," she said when Ski went to open his door. "For some reason Stephanie seems to think you walk on water and I don't want to burst her bubble. You think about what I said and call me when you get it figured out." She scooped up her parcels and pushed the door shut with her hip before Ski could say anything.

He watched her storm up the walk, back stiff with anger. Even after the door slammed shut behind her he sat looking at the duplex. After a couple of minutes he spoke.

"Ho, ho, fucking ho."

Ski's guts were still twisted in anger an hour later when he pulled into Hicks' yard. He barely noticed the kids waving at him as he drove past the house and through the back of their yard to the barnyard. The bitch. All the things he'd done for her and she treated him like that. Forget it. No woman was worth that. He didn't care if she was the first woman he'd ever gone out with who hadn't bored him to tears after a couple of months, or that she made him laugh so easily, or that just being with her and Stephanie seemed to take a weight off his shoulders. Forget that. It didn't make the shit he had to put up worthwhile. Not even close.

Greg was dumping a straw bale over the fence with the front-end loader when Ski pulled up. One already lay on the ground in the pasture. Ski got out of the truck, zipped his coat partway up and put on his gloves. This was just what he needed, even if he was in town clothes. At least Greg was dressed for work, in insulated coveralls and a Polaris toque. Ski waved to Greg as he stomped to the fence and grabbed the pitchfork leaning there.

As Greg wheeled the tractor around and headed back to the stack for another bale, Ski climbed over the fence and attacked the first bale with the pitchfork, tearing huge chunks of straw free and tossing them wide to create a bed for the cattle. By the time Greg dumped the third bale over the fence Ski had almost finished demolishing the first one. He stopped briefly to nod at Greg, then started into the second bale, sweat beading on his brow as he worked, descending into the rhythm of work to overcome his anger. Greg joined him after he'd shut the tractor down, but for once he didn't do his blond Tasmanian Devil routine, pitting his stocky five-foot-six frame against Ski's six feet plus of solid muscle. Instead, Greg just stood back, letting Ski work like a madman and stayed out of the way of the tines on Ski's pitchfork.

"Fastest I've ever gotten this job done," Greg said, as the last bale was reduced to a knee-deep pile of bedding. "You feeling energetic, or does something have you royally pissed off?"

"What do you think?"

"What were you and Terri fighting about now?" Greg asked.

"How – "

Greg snorted, pulled his toque off, scratched his blond hair, then leaned on his pitchfork. "Christ, Ski, you're so transparent you could give glass lessons."

"Yeah, well it shouldn't have been hard to figure out. A woman is the only thing that can piss a guy off that bad and since Terri is the only woman I've seen lately..." Ski shrugged.

"So what's the problem?"

Ski told him.

"Ouch." Greg shook his head. "Did you apologize yet?"

"Apologize?! For what? Christ, it was just a harmless little look."

"Uh-huh. If you're going to keep going out with Terri, the first thing you have to learn is that there is no such thing as a 'harmless little look.' Especially with the way her ex screwed around on her. That'd make anyone paranoid about their boyfriend checking if the grass might not be a little greener on the other side of the fence."

"Like I told her, I'm not her ex-husband. Why should I put up with a bunch of grief because of what he did?" Ski jabbed the pitchfork into the straw. "Maybe I should just break up with her."

"You'd break up with her just because of a little fight?" Greg asked.

"I don't need this shit," Ski said. "There's lots of fish in the sea."

Greg shook his head. "I've heard you say some stupid things over the years, Ski, but that's got to be the stupidest."

Ski glared at Hicks. "What the hell does that mean?"

"It means Terri is the best thing you've ever had going for you. She's smart, good-looking, and for some reason she cares for you. Why would you want to give that up to go back to the bimbo of the week?"

"They weren't bimbos."

"No? My mistake. I just figured because you could

add the IQ of any three of them up to equal Terri's that you might not have been after their minds."

"Why does everyone act like that's such a big deal? Nothing wrong with getting laid a lot."

"Not a thing," Hicks said mildly. "It's just most guys settle down with the same woman for regular sex."

"Yeah? Then how come I keep hearing from all these married guys how the sex stopped for them?" Ski leaned the pitchfork against the fence and stretched. "You hear that joke about the penny jar from Mac's dad?"

Hicks shook his head.

"It goes like this: You get a big jar and put it by your bed when you get married. Every time you have sex in the first year you're married you put a penny into that jar. After the first year, whenever you have sex , you take a penny out. You'll never empty the jar." Ski rubbed his hand over his face. "I prefer adding pennies instead of taking them out."

"That is the biggest crock of shit I've ever heard," Hicks said. "Why the hell would you listen to anything Bill MacAllister said, especially about sex? The man is a sleazebag."

Ski opened his mouth to defend Bill, then stopped. Even Mac would agree with Greg, and it was a rare thing Mac and Greg could agree on.

"I've heard other married guys bitch about not getting any," Ski grumbled.

"Three-hundred-pound assholes," Hicks said. "Sure, there's less sex after awhile, especially when the kids come, but it's not all about sex, you know."

"Why not?" Ski held up his hand before Hicks could

respond. "Forget I asked. I can listen to Terri or watch some chick flick if I want the answer to that again." He rolled his shoulders, stretching the muscles he'd worked. "Want a beer?" he asked.

Hicks looked at his watch. "Did Donna see you drive in?"

"The kids did. I think Donna was in the kitchen when I went by."

"Good. Then she won't be worried when I'm a few minutes late."

Ski shook his head. "See, that's what I mean. A guy can't even have a beer without getting in shit."

It was Hicks' turn to shake his head as they got into Ski's truck.

"Nothing to do with getting shit," he said as Ski started the truck and turned the heater on. "Just don't want her to worry that something happened to me. It's called consideration." He took the beer Ski handed him. "Or does that have too many syllables for you?"

"Fuck you," Ski said, but the words lacked heat. "I can be considerate. I just never thought of Donna worrying about you being hurt."

"That's your problem, Ski. You never think about the little things."

"That's because I don't know about them." Ski slouched in his seat, took a long pull of beer, then wiped the back of his hand across his thick brown moustache. "Christ, it's one thing after another and I've gotten so I feel like I couldn't find my ass with both hands and a map."

"You're in uncharted territory?" Hicks asked.

"Something like that." Ski thought for a moment. "It's like a show I saw when I was babysitting Stephie and Ryan. It was one of these Learning Channel things that Ryan likes." Ski frowned. "Kid can be strange. Anyway, they were talking about these mapmakers, back before Columbus, how when there was some place in the ocean they didn't know anything about they'd draw a sea serpent and write down 'Here be Monsters.' That's what this all feels like for me, that I'm out in the middle of nowhere and every time I turn around another one of those monsters is coming up to bite me on the ass."

Hicks grunted. "So you figure you should head back to familiar ground?"

"Something like that. A lot quieter there."

"A lot more boring too."

"I'll take that chance," Ski said.

"Will you?" Hicks finished his beer and handed the empty to Ski.

"Yeah, sure I will," Ski said, trying to put some conviction into the words.

"And you want me to tell you it's a good idea. Or do you want me to talk you out of it?" Hicks shook his head. "I can't make your mind up for you. All I can do is give you my opinion, and that's that you've got rocks in your head if you dump Terri just because you've got to work at things a bit."

"What does that mean?" Ski said as Hicks climbed out of the truck.

"How can I put it in a way you can understand?" Hicks stood in the open door for a minute, then smiled.

"Got it. Let's just say that giving head isn't the only place where you've got to give a little bit to get a little bit," he said, then slammed the door.

Ski sat silently, a puzzled frown on his face.

Ski wouldn't have believed the mall could be any busier than it had been in the morning, but it was. Of course he also couldn't believe that he'd actually be in the mall twice in one day. Was any woman worth that?

Shit, things couldn't be that bad if he could make bad jokes about them. But if they weren't, why did he still have this knot in his gut? And why was he sitting here in the food court, trying to figure out what Terri meant, what Greg meant? He'd hoped returning to the scene of the crime might make things a bit clearer, but all it did was make it harder to think. At least Terri was only a few minutes away if he did get things figured out. Didn't seem likely that he was going to though. Why couldn't he have his cake and eat it too? He always had before. And that whole giving-head thing just didn't make sense. Yeah, you'd give a little head to get a little head.

He shrugged. He could think about that later. For now he'd just think about Terri. Wasn't like she was hard to look at. Sure, she wasn't one of those Hollywood types that weighed a hundred pounds, ten of it tits. No, Terri looked like a real woman. Not Heather Locklear, but more like Loni Anderson with long brown hair and a lot more brains. But her body was only what got his attention at first. What kept it were her eyes and laugh. He'd always heard about flashing eyes, sparkling eyes, but he hadn't really understood what the terms meant until he saw the way Terri's brown eyes could shift in mood, playing with him one minute, pinning him to the wall the next. And her laugh. No girlish giggle there, but a full, deep laugh that he'd been able to hear clearly across a noisy bar the first night he met her. When she was having fun she wasn't afraid to show it. She'd told him once that if she didn't have at least three good belly laughs on a first date, then she knew the guy wasn't for her.

He stared down into his coffee cup. Sure Terri was fun to be with and a real smartass, but was that worth changing who he was? He took a drag on his cigarette. Shit, he'd quit smoking in his own house so the smell wouldn't bother Stephie's asthma. That was giving a little bit, wasn't it? And he'd been faithful. What else did she want from him? Jesus, he talked to her a lot, went to most of Stephie's activities, and even put up with her loser brother-in-law when she and Tanya went out. That had to be at least halfway to meeting her. What did she give when he did all that?

He sipped his coffee. He knew the answer, even if he didn't want to admit it. Lots, she gave lots. She'd help with the chores when she came to the farm, she'd brought Tanya out and they'd gone over his house from top to bottom, she was being a good sport about trying to learn to ride a horse. No, he couldn't lie to himself. She was adjusting to the farm, adjusting to him, trying to build something that might last. He saw her doing all that. Was it too much to ask that he take a step toward halfway? Shit, she wanted a boyfriend who wasn't always looking around, who didn't stare at other women. How tough could that be to give her? It was Christmas after all, and maybe it wouldn't come with a bow on it, but it'd be a lot better gift than a blender or another sweater. Besides, it was the gift that kept on giving. She'd get a well-behaved boyfriend and he'd get some peace and quiet. He was willing to give that little bit to get that little bit.

He nodded firmly. That was the answer. He'd quit looking at other women. This was the perfect place to practise, too. Lots of women walking around and some had taken their parkas off while they shopped. He'd watch from here for a while and practise, then he could go for a stroll around the mall, not looking at women.

Like taking candy from a baby.

He scanned the crowd for a likely practise babe. Didn't want to start off too gorgeous. Start with just okay and work his way up, that was the way. Like a kid. Crawl first, then walk, then run. A little bit of practise and he'd be ready to take Terri shopping tomorrow.

There. A bit older than him, but not bad. As good a place to start as any. The hard-body twenty-year-olds could wait an hour or so.

The woman was browsing in the window of a men's wear store. When she walked away he'd just keep his head pointed straight ahead. Do that a few times, then go for a stroll.

When she walked away, he stared straight ahead. Nothing to it. Sure he felt like someone had jammed a crowbar up his ass all the way to the top of his skull, but that feeling should go away after a while.

He hoped.

Okay, that was one. Next up. This time he went for one around his age. Pretty enough, but could stand to lose a few pounds. This one was going to be tougher. What else could he do besides looking straight ahead? Focus on a part of her body that didn't turn him on? What did that leave, her feet?

He shook his head. Concentrate. She walked away and he stared straight ahead again. Two times. He could do this. But he'd been sitting here too long. Time to move on.

He started down the main corridor of the mall. Nothing really to look at. All parkas and long coats. Then he saw a blonde coming toward him. Five eight, maybe a hundred and ten. Black turtleneck and jeans. If he could avoid checking out the back view on her, he had this not-looking thing cased. He just had to concentrate, to look straight ahead.

She sailed by him, smiling.

His head turned.

"You want me to do what?" Hicks' voice was incredulous through the earpiece of the telephone.

"I want you to come into Prince Albert and teach me how not to look at women," Ski said. "What part of that don't you understand?"

"I understand what you said. I just can't see how the hell you figure I'd be able to teach you something like that."

"You're smart; you'll figure something out."

"You're fucking insane, Ski."

"No need to swear," Ski said. "I'm just asking for a favour." His voice lowered, became wheedling. "You said you wanted me and Terri to stay together, didn't you?"

"Well, yeah..."

"And you said I should learn to give a little bit, didn't you?"

"Yeah, but – "

"Well this is where I decided to start giving a bit, but I can't do it without your help."

There was silence on the other end of the line.

"Greg? You still there?"

"Yeah. Man, I've got to be almost as stunned as you are to even be thinking about this." He sighed loudly. "Give me one good reason why I should do this."

"Because you like Terri and this would be your Christmas present to her."

"I'd sooner give her a box of Turtles," Hicks said dryly.

"C'mon, Greg, I'm begging you. Please..."

"Christ, okay, but what am I going to tell Donna when she asks what the rush is to go to town?"

"Tell her the truth. Sorta. Tell her I'm on Terri's shit list and I'm trying to get off it by sucking up and buying her something nice. Tell her I'm worried that Terri will be really pissed if I wait till tomorrow to do this."

"You expect her to buy that? Ski, she's never seen you that worried about all the other women you've dated combined. Come to think about it, neither have I.

What *is* the big rush to do this tonight?"

Ski drummed his fingers on the side of the phone. How to explain this?

"It's not just for Terri," he finally admitted. "It pisses me off that I can't do something simple like keep my eyes to myself. It's gnawing at me. Every other guy in the world seems to be able to do this, so why not me?"

"Good question. Okay, I'll help you on one condition. You can't tell anybody about this."

"Who would I tell? Mac or Ken? I can just hear Mac: 'I can't believe it, you're actually taking lessons on how to be pussy-whipped.' No thanks. You don't have to worry about me saying anything."

"I can hear MacAllister too," Hicks said. "Mum's the word, then. Does this really have to be tonight, though?"

"Yeah, I gotta prove to myself that I can do this."

Hicks sighed again. "Okay, I still haven't bought Donna her present so it won't be a totally wasted trip. Meet me in the food court in an hour."

"Thanks. I owe you one."

"Ain't that the truth."

"I still can't believe I let you talk me into this," Hicks said as he dropped onto the chair across from Ski and unzipped his ski jacket. "I think I let all this 'goodwill toward men' stuff get to me."

"'Tis the season for giving,'" Ski said.

"Yeah, right. Look, what exactly do you want?"

"Like I told you on the phone. Show me how to look at a woman without getting caught."

"That's not what you said. You just wanted to learn how not to look. Why not just quit looking?" Hicks' smile sharpened.

"Don't bust my balls. You know that's not natural." Ski frowned at Hicks. "You still look, don't you?"

"Sometimes."

"And Donna doesn't catch you, does she?"

"No, but even if she did, she knows she can trust me. The eyes may wander a bit, but she knows I won't."

"You know I only go with one woman at a time," Ski said. "Everyone around Pine Valley knows that. Christ, your wife even told Terri that."

"I know and maybe Terri even knows that in her head, but it hasn't been long enough for her to believe it deep down inside."

"That's why I need your help," Ski said. "If Terri doesn't see me looking at other women for a while, maybe she'll stop being so paranoid. Who knows, maybe I'll even be able to quit looking so much after a while."

"I suppose it's possible, but it sounds more like you're trying to convince yourself it might happen than it being what you really think."

Ski shrugged. "As long as it gets the job done I don't care."

"It's your life," Hicks said, taking a sip of his coffee. "You sure you want to do this? It could be the first step on a slippery slope. Who knows, maybe in a few months you'll be totally domesticated."

"You mean pussy-whipped. Not bloody likely."

Hicks smiled. "Don't be too sure of that."

Ski's eyes narrowed. "Are you here to pick my ass or you going to help me?"

"Picking on you is more fun, but I said I'd help, so let's do it."

"Good." Ski leaned forward, eyes intent. "Where do we start?"

"Good question. I thought about it on the way in and didn't come up with much. It's not like there's a handbook on this or anything." Hicks leaned back in his chair. "Probably best if I just watch what you do when a woman walks by and see what happens. Then we can go from there." He looked at the crowd flowing by. "There, the one in the brown leather jacket, with the red headband. Check her out."

Ski looked at the woman, conscious of Hicks' eyes on him. She was a good choice, not too flashy, mid-twenties, a nice little wiggle when she walked.

"Christ, no wonder Terri's pissed with you, " Greg said.

Ski's head snapped back. "What?"

"I thought you were going to pull an *Exorcist* there. I thought your head was going to spin all the way around," Hicks said.

"C'mon, it wasn't that bad."

"Yes it was." Hicks frowned. "I knew you were bad for that when we were out alone, but I thought maybe you were a bit smarter with Terri."

"You're not serious are you? I didn't do anything really bad there, did I?"

"Are you listening to me? Yes, you were very obvious." Hicks smiled. "But that gives me your first rule. 'Never turn your head to look at another woman.'"

"Never?"

"Is there an echo in here? Never. Zero. Zilch. Not until the end of time." Hicks leaned forward. "If you don't listen to anything else I tell you, listen to that."

"If I can't move my head, how am I going to see anything?" Ski asked plaintively.

"You sound like one of my kids when I tell them they can't have any candy," Hicks said.

"Well, it's so stupid – "

"Do you want me to keep helping you with this or not," Hicks snapped.

"Yes," Ski said, resigned. He slumped in his chair. "It's not a natural thing to do, that's all I'm saying."

"I can see I'm going to have to put this in ways even you can understand," Hicks said. He sat silently for a minute. "Okay, here's how you've got to think of it. When we're out in the bush deer hunting, what does the deer do that gives it away and gets it shot?"

"It moves," Ski said immediately. His eyes widened. Holy shit. That made sense.

"That's right," Hicks said. "Just think of yourself as a deer and Terri as a hunter with a really big gun."

"I can do that," Ski said slowly. "But how can she see that all the time?"

Hicks thought for a second again. "Think of a baseball game," he said. "There's a runner on first and the pitcher is checking him out. Does he have to turn his whole head to watch the runner?"

"Nah, the corner of his eye is all he..."

"The light bulb finally goes on," Hicks said.

"This is great," Ski said. "What else is there?"

"Jeez, that should be enough to keep you out of trouble for a while."

"Maybe, but I want to learn it all."

"Ski, I don't even know what all there is to tell you. It's not like my dad took me aside and showed me this or I took a class in university." Hicks rubbed his hand over his face. "I don't know if I even should've told you what I did. It feels like a cheat. You should have to work at this like the rest of us did. How can you have a real relationship if you won't do the work?"

"Don't get touchy-feely on me, Greg. For me, this is work. I'm just so far behind I need a tutor."

"You need your head examined." Hicks held up his hand to stop Ski's reply. "I know, you're doing this for Terri." He sighed. "Let's get this over with. Another easy one is sunglasses, but you can figure that out on your own." He drummed his fingers on the table. "You can turn your whole body and pretend to look at something else. Make sure there's really something there, though, and don't look straight at the woman."

"So the corner of the eye works for me like it does for Terri?"

"Give the man a gold star."

"But what am I supposed to look at?" Ski asked.

"Like teaching a mule," Hicks grumbled. "I should've brought a two-by-four to whack you between the eyes with."

"That's only to get the mule's attention," Ski said. "Now, you've got my attention, so tell me what you mean."

"Look over there." Hicks pointed at the men's wear store where Ski's first practice woman had been browsing. "Does anything there catch your eye? And I don't mean a woman."

Ski looked at the store. "Well, that's got to be one of the ugliest colours for a suit I've ever seen. And there's a sale at the bookstore next door. Terri'd like that."

"Very good," Hicks said. "What else did you see?"

"The tight-bodied teenybopper and the stacked redhead."

"Didn't think you'd miss them, but your eyes flicked toward them. Wasn't much, but if Terri was watching you, she'd notice." Hicks looked around. "Check out the food stands over there."

Ski turned his head slowly, looking at the A&W, the sub shop, the pizza place.

"So what do you want to eat?" Hicks asked.

"The blonde eating pizza," Ski said.

Hicks jerked his head around. "Not bad. I didn't even notice her and your eyes never twitched."

"That's all there is to it?" Ski smiled.

"Don't ask me. It's all I can think of. Or want to think of. You're on your own from here on in."

"Can't you stay around so I can practise?"

"You know how much I hate this fucking mall," Hicks said. "And I told Donna I wouldn't be long."

"Say you were looking for her Christmas present. Or helping me with Terri's. That's the truth."

"What if she asks me what you bought?"

"Don't know. That's something else we've got to do."

"Ski..."

"Relax. I'll make it worth your while."

"How?"

"We can bet for chores. Usual stakes. You catch me looking, you get a day. I get away with one, I get a day."

"Winner picks the days?" Hicks said.

Ski nodded. It meant that one of them would be doing the other's chores at forty below, but he didn't intend to lose.

Hicks grinned. "Let's get going then." He rubbed his hands together. "Like money in the bank," he said.

Ski bit his lip. He was so fucking sick of this mall and all the people in it. Three trips in two days were three too many. But he'd got Greg to help him pick out a sweater for Terri's sister and he'd used that as a peace offering to Terri. Of course, she thought it wasn't right for Tanya and they'd had to return it, but it softened her up enough that Ski could buy her brunch, and things were slightly better. She was watching him like a hawk, though, and wasn't talking to him any more than necessary, but at least she was talking and they'd agreed to get another sweater for Tanya.

"Is it going to be a problem taking you into the stores with me?" Terri said, her voice cool. "I know just how safe it is leaving you outside."

"Outside, inside, it doesn't matter. Just as long as I don't have to try on any of the clothes we should be all right."

"I don't think you're Tanya's size," Terri said dryly. "Something to do with the eight-inch height difference."

"And things being built a bit different."

"That too." Terri stopped outside one of the few stores they hadn't been in and looked at the brightly dressed mannequins in the window. "They might have something in here."

Ski bit his lip. Must be hundreds of sweaters in each store. Surely Tanya would like at least one of those. But he stayed silent. No arguments today. He'd even keep the smart-ass comments to a minimum. Couldn't cut them out totally or Terri would think he was up to something. No, today he was on his best behaviour.

"Yeah, they might have a sweater or two," he said and followed Terri into the store to a table full of sweaters. As she sorted through them he looked around for a second. Then Terri looked up.

Shit.

"Something wrong," Terri said, ice in her voice.

"Just making sure no one I know will see me in here," he said.

She rolled her eyes. "Grow up," she said, her voice only a touch warmer.

"Yes ma'am." Ski grinned. "I guess it could be worse. We could be in the underwear section of one of the department stores."

"Lingerie, Ski." Her voice was almost amused. "Call it lingerie and you won't feel so embarrassed."

"As long as we're not going there today." It'd been bad enough when Greg had dragged him there last night to look for something for Donna. Ski had known better than to buy something for Terri there. That'd be a gift more for him and he didn't want to piss her off even more.

"No, Ski, I won't put you through that today." The corners of her mouth twitched. "But if you do act up, I'll make you hold my purse."

"Terri..."

"Man, you are pathetic." Terri turned back to the sweaters, grinning slightly.

Ski smothered a grin of his own. That was more like the old Terri. Maybe yesterday wouldn't stay around to bother them for as long as he thought. He stepped up to the table, dug through a pile of sweaters. He caught a glimpse of long blonde hair out of the corner of his eye. He stopped his head from turning just in time.

Okay, this'd be the perfect opportunity to see if Greg had taught him anything and to see if he could stay off Terri's shit list.

"How about that sweater over there?" he said, pointing to one on a half-mannequin.

Terri looked up. "Christ, Ski, Tanya wouldn't be caught dead in that."

"Why not? It's a really bright colour and that's the kind of thing she really likes."

"It looks like acrylic," Terri said. "Don't you know anything about fashion?" She held up a hand before he could reply. "I know, stupid question. Thanks for trying though."

"No problem." Ski dropped his gaze. Blonde had been not bad. Fresh looking, cheeks red like she'd just come in from the cold. Sweet. And he'd seen all he'd needed to without Terri noticing or being hurt. Greg had done a good job and Ski had done what Greg said. He'd given a little bit to get a little bit. Sure, he was cheating, but it was for her, not on her. It was a white lie kind of cheating, not like what her ex-husband had done. Yeah, that's the way it was.

Sure it was.

HUSTLE

I breathed a sigh of relief when we walked into the Maddin Hotel bar. Only two other guys in it and I didn't know them. Nothing to keep Mac here for more than a couple of beers. Or to get him into trouble. Babysitting him should be easy for once.

"Shit, this place is dead," Mac said. "We should have stayed in Melfort, Ken."

"Why," I said, more harshly than I intended. "Everyone else from Pine Valley went home after the auction. Why the hell shouldn't we?"

Mac's eyebrows lifted in surprise. "Hey, don't bite my head off because all the equipment you wanted went high. There's lots of auctions for Christ sake, especially now. Just keep your eyes open." He sank down into one of the heavy captain's chairs that were Maddin's trademark and sighed. "Most comfortable chairs anywhere down the line."

"Yeah," I said, dropping into a chair myself. They were the only thing that distinguished Maddin from any of a dozen bars Mac and I had been to. Same rack of chips and Cheesies by the bar. Same Hot Rods and beef jerky up by the pickled eggs. Even the same poster of some blonde with a Canadian in her hand and her tits stretching an undersized T-shirt, nipples on high-beam. Déja vu all over again, as Yogi Berra said. Except for the chairs. High-backed, thickly upholstered, if they had a footstool, a guy would think he was at home. Which wouldn't be a bad idea.

"Christ, Ken, quit sulking. There's at least three more big auctions this summer and you might get lucky at one of the smaller sales. Besides," he said, taking off his cap and running his fingers through his sandy hair, "you should be worrying about harvest now, not seed-ing."

"I've already got everything ready," I said as the wait-ress finally pulled her ass away from the video lottery terminal where she'd been watching the other guys play. "Two Pilsner," I said.

"Make that a double vodka and Coke for me," Mac said. Shit, just what I needed, Mac on war juice. His face was already flushed from nipping at a bottle with some of the old guys at the auction but I hoped it wouldn't get him on a hard-stuff night. He was always easier to get along with on beer. Not easy, necessarily, just easier.

"So, how are things going with Carol?" Mac asked. "She figured out what she's got herself into yet?"

"You're a bundle of laughs, Mac. And things are going great. She's got a stagette to go to tonight so we're not getting together until tomorrow night."

"Never thought I'd see the day that a blind date Radinski set up would work out." He laughed. It brought a hint of softness to the hard lines of his face. "Or even be human."

I chuckled. "No shit. But it wasn't a blind date. We just met at that party at Terri's last month."

"Yeah right, and Ski and Terri didn't set it up? C'mon Ken, get real. You were set up. Admit it."

"No."

"Why not?"

"Cause Carol has a brain and Ski never introduced me to a woman with a brain before." I smiled. "Just big breasts."

"Yeah, Ski and big tits. Like bacon and eggs." Mac took a swig of his drink and chuckled. "You remember those twins from Prince Albert that Ski was chasing? God, I never seen such huge knockers in my life."

"And small brains."

"And quick hands. Poor Ski went a month without so much as a feel, let alone anything else. Thought he was going to explode from come buildup."

I laughed. This might be all right after all. Keep Mac on the old stories and it'd be a quiet night.

"Yeah, that was the longest he went without since the railroad. Of course I don't remember you doing any better with either – "

"Hey guys, how's it going?" One of the guys from the VLTs stood a few feet from our table. "My buddy and I were wondering if you'd like to shoot some pool."

"We were – " I started, before Mac butted in.

"Sure. Any stakes or just for fun?"

"How about first game for fun, then we'll see?" He rolled the cue ball around on the pool table. He was a big guy, heavy through the shoulders and chest and with a gut hanging over his belt. A plaid work shirt with the sleeves cut off covered a black Black Sabbath T-shirt and he wore well-used workboots. The steel toes showed through the worn leather. He had a thick moustache and thick eyebrows. He looked like a heavy metal Joseph Stalin. He also looked like he'd seen a few fights. Mac was over six feet, but he was leaner, and he carried the marks from when he went up against guys Stalin's size, especially the bump on his nose from it getting broken.

"Our table from before, so we break," Stalin said.

"Sure." Mac started to get up.

"Thanks for asking if I wanted to play," I said.

"Oh, lighten up. We can talk about the old days any-time. Wait till we get back to Pine Valley." He lowered his voice. "Besides, we can probably take a few bucks off these shitheads."

Great. Just fucking great. Mac and pool. Again, just what I needed. If Ski and big tits were bacon and eggs, Mac, pool and fights were a hamburger, fries and gravy. They just went together naturally. Give me a break. I was getting my shit together; why couldn't Mac?

Stalin broke and the thirteen went down. "We're high," he said as he chalked up his cue for his second shot. Like we didn't know that. I sipped my beer and looked at the waitress. Cute little thing. Young too. Twenty-one tops. Way too young and inexperienced to head trouble off before it happened. Too interested in the VLTs anyway. Would've been nice to have a Brenda type in here. Or even in Pine Valley still. She would've read things and had the cops "accidentally" walking in, or jumped in when things got too intense. This little blonde was just too interested in dropping quarters into the money pit. I'd heard her arguing strategies with Stalin earlier. Like you could out-think a machine. God knows I'd tried when they first came out, but after a little while the thrill had worn off. Guess I was lucky. Mac still figured he could come out ahead and get money for nothing.

Stalin blew a fairly easy straight shot into the corner pocket, shook his head and stepped back from the table.

"Fucking thing just doesn't have the runs in it like the one back home."

"Yeah," Mac said as he lined up the four, "but it's more fun that way." He sank it easily, then followed up quickly with the seven and the two. He started whistling as he chalked up his cue for his fourth shot. Not good. He was getting cocky and that always screwed up his game. It also made him that much more pissed off when he started losing. Sure enough it was his turn to blow a fairly easy shot, bouncing the five off the side a couple of inches from the pocket.

"Too bad," said Stalin's partner, some blond-haired cowboy type in a faded jean jacket and beat-up straw hat. Guy looked like he'd seen that James Dean poster, the one where he's a cowboy. Somebody should've told him that acne and all the scars it'd left and a honking big Adam's apple kind of ruined the cool effect he was trying for. Even the cigarette hanging from the corner of his mouth didn't help. He banked the eleven in, then did a combination to put the fifteen down. His next bank shot fell short though. My turn.

The table was fairly open now, with the eight up against the rail by the far end. I lined up the three, aiming for about half the ball to cut it in. A smooth tap and in. Now I had shape on the six and it went straight down. The one was hidden behind the fourteen and the five was tight to the rail so I just gave the one a kiss to leave it in the open for Mac.

The other guys looked at each other, then Stalin tried a bank on the nine. "Shit," he said, bouncing his cue off the table as the nine hit a couple of inches from the side pocket. "Sorry," he said to his buddy. Dean just shrugged.

Mac was grinning when he got up to shoot, his drink empty in front of him. I bit my lip as he cleaned the table off with quick sure strokes, his cockiness not affecting his skill anymore.

"Another one? Maybe for a drink this time?" he asked and Stalin nodded, his heavy brows shading unreadable brown eyes.

"Sure, we got time." He put his quarters in and started racking the balls as they tumbled into the slot. Mac waved at the waitress.

"Two more." I looked at my almost full beer. Another one of *those* nights.

"Not for me," I said, surprising myself.

Mac frowned. "Don't be a fucking wimp."

"I've got a full one." The smile was gone from Mac's face. "The cops are going to be watching for people coming back pissed from the sale and I don't need an impaired."

"Afraid it'll fuck up your love life?" Mac said, still not smiling.

"That's a good enough reason. And maybe I just don't want one." Mac's eyes narrowed at this and he tried to stare me down.

Not this time.

We stayed like that for a couple of seconds until the waitress broke in. "So should I get the beer or not?"

"Fuck it," Mac said, looking away. "If he wants to be a candy-ass let him." He got up and walked to the pool table, his face tight as he drove his cue forward. He caught the cue ball low and hard and it bounced off the table when it hit the triangle of balls.

"Fuck," Mac said, his face red.

Stalin shook his head. "Tough break. Costs a dollar too."

"What?"

"They've got a kitty. Buck a ball bounced off the table. Goes to whoever sinks the eight off the break." He grimaced. "We already gave someone a couple bucks today."

Mac looked at the waitress who pointed to the clearly labelled jar on the bar. He shrugged, yanked a loonie out of his pocket and tossed it into the jar with the dozen or so already in there. "Shoot already," he said to the big guy, the red still high on his cheeks.

"Yeah, relax." Stalin set the cue ball to one side of centre in line with the seven and dropped it. As he walked around the table chalking up his cue I tried to calm Mac down.

"Jeez, Mac, you're turning into Darchuk knocking balls off the table like that." I managed a weak chuckle. "Remember that time Ski was stupid enough to stand at the end of the table when Darchuk was breaking. Nothing like a pool ball in the nuts to ruin your night."

"I ain't fucking Darchuk."

Something snapped. I'd ignored Mac's worsening moods for long enough, taken his shit and tried to understand. No more.

"No, he has a fucking brain and doesn't get pissed off everytime he turns around."

He started to reply, then stopped when Stalin missed the three. "Shoot," he said flatly.

Fuck it. I got up and nailed the fourteen hard, then sat down while it was still bouncing from side to side.

"Do I have to do everything myself?" Mac asked.

"Be about time you did something for yourself."

His hand tightened on his glass and I got ready to duck. I'd seen the glass-and-bottle-throwing trick before, but never from the receiving end. I didn't care though. I'd hustled off and on the farm over the last year to try and get my shit together. I'd had a lot of help from friends. I figured I owed Mac at least that but he just didn't want to listen. If I was this bad Ski or Brenda should have smacked me one. Instead I had Mac wanting to hit me.

"Go ahead," I said, "lose it on the only friend you've got left."

"I've got lots of friends."

"Beer buddies aren't friends. They'd drop you in a second to save themselves trouble. Damn it, even Ski's given up on you. I'm all you got left." I relaxed, letting myself sprawl in my chair. "Take your shot if you want to, but for once think about how much it's going to cost you."

Mac's lips were a thin white line, the rest of his face flushed red. I kept my gaze steady on him until he looked away toward Stalin and Dean.

"What the fuck are you looking at?" Mac snapped. The cowboy's face reddened.

"Just wondering if we're still playing," the big guy said mildly, seemingly unimpressed by Mac's anger.

"Yeah, we're fucking playing," Mac said, jerking himself to his feet. "You guys are one ball up so how's about we bump the stakes to five bucks a piece."

Stalin and Dean looked at each other and Dean smiled briefly. "Sure, five bucks it is," he said.

I looked at Mac and swallowed my outburst. He was on the edge, ready to swing at anyone. Maybe winning a game would cool him off. Even if I had a bad feeling about it. These guys were too cool, too relaxed. They'd been here before, but they were missing too many easy shots for two guys who'd spent that much time in the bar. And they were way too ready to raise the stakes. Shit was going down.

Again.

And I sat doing nothing.

Again.

Mac took an easy shot on the eleven, bouncing it into the pocket as he shot hard. He took a couple of deep breaths, then lightly kissed the fifteen into the side pocket. A combo on the fourteen and a bank on the nine and we had control. The red was fading from Mac's face as a tough cut on the thirteen just failed to go down.

"Left you nothing but easy stuff," Mac said as he handed me the cue. "Easiest money you made in a long time."

"Maybe," I said as the big guy dropped the two. "But something stinks here." The four went down.

"Like what?" Mac asked as the six came up short on the light tap in.

I shrugged. They weren't missing anything that any of us don't miss one time or another, but the timing seemed funny. I got up and sank the thirteen that Mac had left by the hole. He was waving for another double as I did a long combination on the ten. Only the twelve and the eight left. I tried a double bank on the twelve, ending up just by a corner pocket. Stalin frowned and whispered something to Dean. The cowboy nodded. I stayed standing as he dropped the three in the side, then came up light on the five, leaving Mac an easy shot on the twelve and nice shape on the eight.

I frowned. The five had been a stupid shot. He should've tried the seven. That way if he missed, Mac would've had a tough shot on the twelve. Instead, Mac took the cue from me and sank the two balls easily.

"See, I told you, easy money," he said just loud enough so they'd have to hear.

Dean reddened again but Stalin just smiled. They dropped their fives on the table.

"How about we make the next one really interesting if it's such easy money?" Stalin asked. "How about twenty bucks each next game?"

"Sure – "

"Mac!" I hissed, grabbing the cue in his hand. He ignored me.

"I'll cover it even if Ken won't," he said. Stalin shrugged and plugged his quarters into the table. As the balls rumbled down, I used the noise to cover my whispers to Mac.

"Mac, they're hustling us."

"No shit." He shook his head at me. "I wasn't born yesterday."

"But – "

"We can take them." He yanked the cue away from me.

On the table maybe, I thought, as Mac lined up his first shot, but what about after? Stalin was way bigger than either of us, probably over two-fifty with that gut, and Dean was a wiry six feet. If he was as fast as he looked he'd give Mac a lot of trouble and I'd be fucked. Actually, I was fucked either way as I didn't figure I'd last more than one punch against Stalin, not when he outweighed me by a good eighty pounds. The waitress had finally looked up from the VLT when she'd heard twenty bucks but all she'd done was go behind the bar. A cordless phone sat by her hand and I figured the cops were on the speed dial and it wasn't like they were twenty miles away like in Pine Valley. Nope, five minutes from the nearest RCMP detachment to here.

"Table's still open," Mac said, as the balls rolled to a stop. Good break though, with the balls scattered around the table. We were all standing around the table now and I'd taken a cue from the rack. Damned if I knew if it was straight or not, but it had a good weight to it. Stalin took a long look, then shot the three into the corner pocket. Whistling as he chalked up his cue, he walked around the table and banked the seven in. A combination and the four went down. No mistakes now. The five was barely visible behind the fourteen and he just caught it, putting it into the side. Mac's eyes were on the cowboy now, narrow and watchful.

The big guy had no real shot now, so he banked the six off the side. It hit the twelve and missed the pocket. Stalin stepped silently back from the table.

I surveyed the table as I tried to decide what to do. Blow the game and to hell with the money? Let Mac be pissed off with me. It was better than another fight. No real help from anyone in the room. The waitress would wait till things started before calling the cops and by then it would be too late. I looked at Mac as I slowly chalked my cue. Him and the cowboy were staring at each other. Great. Me and Stalin.

Fuck it.

I tossed my cue onto the table, knocking a couple of balls out of the way. "This is bullshit. You stupid bastards want to play your little games, go right ahead but leave me out of it." I looked at the waitress. "If you want to save yourself a lot of trouble, you should phone the cops right now."

"Ken – "

"What kind of bullshit is this?" Stalin said. He smiled at the waitress. "The guy doesn't know what the hell he's talking about, so why don't you just put the phone down and relax." Suddenly she looked fifteen years old, a kid trying to play at adult. The big son of a bitch had to make two and a half of her. She put the phone down and clenched her trembling hands together. Stalin smiled and looked at Mac. "This is just a friendly game of pool, right?"

"Yeah, that's right, " Mac said, taking his eyes off Dean long enough to smile at the waitress too. "We're just going to spot the balls where they were and I'll play for both of us."

"The asshole's money stays in," the cowboy said.

"Yeah, but you're not going to see it, crater-face." Mac was still smiling as he looked back at the cowboy, who straightened from the table he'd been resting against. Dean stubbed out his cigarette.

"Watch it, asshole."

I winced, waiting for the comeback that was sure to set things off. Instead, Mac just smiled that crazy smile of his and leaned over the table, his cue lining up, the balls clicking as the ten went down.

"After I take your money," Mac said, sinking the thirteen. "Then we'll see who's the asshole."

I stood at our table, coat in hand. Leave, stay, the conflicting messages bounced around my head. I tried, I told myself, but I knew better. It was like every other time, too little, too late. So did I hang around like a good little friend and clean up Mac's mess – if I survived Stalin – or did I walk and let Mac take a beating? Might knock some sense into him, though losing a fight had never helped before. Besides, I couldn't be sure when the other two would stop, or even if they would. And Mac had a pool cue in his hands. Stalin's skull didn't look that thick. I looked at the waitress. Her face was white and she had her bottom lip clamped tightly in her teeth. She was safe though. Just scared. I didn't owe her anything.

The fifteen dropped.

I took a step toward the door.

Combination. The nine went down.

I stepped back, looked at the poor waitress.

Bank. The twelve.

Mac smiled and did a Tom Cruise, waving the cue behind his back and tucking it under his arm.

Stalin and Dean stepped closer to the table.

Heart pounding, I walked the ten feet to the bar and picked up the phone. The cops were number one on the speed dial. I hit it.

"No one is in the detachment at this time," a computer said. "Your call is being forwarded to – "

Stalin yanked the phone from my hand and hit the off button. He crowded me back against the bar. "Stay out of this, asshole," he said, his beery breath hot on my face. One thing I learned from Mac: if a fight is going to happen anyway – and this one was no matter who won the game – then get the first shot in. Especially if you're out of your league.

I drove my knee as hard as I could into Stalin's nuts.

His eyes widened and he lunged at me, big arms spread wide. I ducked sideways, grabbed the phone out of his hand and threw it to the waitress. There was yelling and the sound of blows behind me, but Mac could take care of himself. As Stalin turned, right hand cupping his groin, I punched him as hard as I could in the face. Pain flared in my knuckles and then he caught me with a swinging left arm and I stumbled backwards. He stayed on his feet, bent over and breathing rapidly.

I risked a quick glance. Shit. The cowboy was as fast as he looked and he wasn't stupid enough to go toe to toe with Mac. The booze had slowed Mac down and Dean was landing good punches while Mac missed on his much harder shots. Shit, shit, shit.

I swung around and saw Stalin straightening. Christ, what'd the guy have, stainless steel nuts? Run away, run away, a voice yelled in my head. Instead, I grabbed Mac's drink and threw it in Stalin's face. He stopped and pawed at his face as the vodka stung his eyes. I faked another kick at his balls and he stepped backwards. Should've brought the pool cue with you, the little voice said, as Stalin lumbered forward. No shit. I spun one of the heavy chairs in front of him and backpedalled rapidly. He knocked the chair away and came even faster. I reached the pool table, grabbed a cue. Stalin stopped, shaking his head and swaying sideways, waiting for me to commit. I backed around the table. Waitress was yelling into the phone. I hoped the cops weren't too far away.

Out of the corner of my eye I could see where Dean had backed Mac up against the VLTs and was looping haymakers against Mac's arms where they were up in front of his face. Good. Mac was playing rope-a-dope and had the cowboy where he wanted him. Sure enough, Dean stepped in for a better shot and Mac lunged forward, grabbing the collar of his jean jacket. His fist smacked into the cowboy's face, blood flying as Dean's nose broke.

"Motherfucker!" Stalin lunged toward me. I swung, the cue bouncing harmlessly off a raised arm. I saw a huge fist coming and managed to duck just enough so it didn't take my head off. Lights flared as the fist bounced off the top of my head. I went down, seeing Stalin's boots as he stepped over me. I knew I should grab him but nothing seemed to work. I lay on the floor, looking under the end of the pool table. I could see Dean lying face down on the floor ten feet away, a pool of blood soaking the carpet by his head. I could hear yelling and the sound of blows, but it seemed a long ways away. I tried my legs again. Movement. Slowly I rolled to my knees, pulled myself up with the help of the pool table.

I should've stayed on the floor.

Mac and Stalin were hammering at each other, both bloody, shirts ripped. Mac was backed up against the pool table. Stalin lunged forward, pinning Mac to the table and grabbing his right arm. The big man drew his fist back as Mac jabbed weakly at him with his left hand. I started staggering toward them. Stalin's fist smacked into Mac's face. Mac's left hand scrabbled around on the table, grabbed a pool ball. He brought it looping into the side of Stalin's head. Stalin's fist dropped. Mac swung again, the pock of pool ball on head loud in the suddenly quiet bar. Stalin stumbled back, his eyes glazed. Mac drove a right into the big man's face and he went down. Then Mac was on top of him, fist flashing up, down, up, down, into his defenceless face.

"Mac, no," I croaked. I tottered toward them, the ten feet taking forever. Up, down, up, down. I grabbed his arm as it came up. He swung around, eyes wild.

"You won, Mac, you won." I held on to his arm, talking calmly, talking him down like a wild horse. "Easy now." I pulled him away from Stalin. "Easy." He slumped into a chair, picked up Dean's beer, drained it.

I knelt by Stalin. Jesus. Blood and bruises. Not a single patch of uninjured skin on his face. Nose broken too. He coughed, blood splattering from his mouth.

"Mac, give me a hand. We've got to turn him over or he'll choke to death."

"Fuck him. We've got to get out of here." He waved toward the waitress. "The little bitch called the cops. Let's go."

I looked at him, seeing him for the first time the way he was now, not the way I wanted him to be from the past. Any kindness was gone. All he had left was anger. And fear. Though he'd never admit that.

"Run if you want to, Mac. There's nowhere far enough."

"What the fuck are you talking about? We gotta go."

I ignored him, straining with weakened arms to roll Stalin over. Suddenly the waitress was there, pulling while I pushed. Slowly the big man rolled to his side. Blood dribbled out of his mouth.

"Good girl." I smiled at her, pleased she had some colour back in her face. "It's okay, it's all over. Now will you do something for me?" She nodded, watching Mac like you'd watch a rabid dog. "Good. Call an ambulance and then get me some towels soaked in cold water. Can you do that for me?" She nodded again and walked to the bar.

Suddenly Mac grabbed me by the collar and yanked me to my feet. "Are you through playing boy scout? The cops could be here anytime. Let's get the fuck out of here."

I slapped his hand away. "Go if you want. I'm staying."

His face tightened. "Fine. Be that fucking way. Just give me the car keys."

"No"

Mac pushed me back into the pool table. "Give me the fucking keys."

"No."

"Damn it..."

"There's only one way to get the keys from me, Mac. Start swinging. I won't stop you."

"Ken – " the cry tore from his throat.

"I'm sorry, Mac." I pushed past him, opened the door. A police siren was clear in the distance. "Your call, Mac. Take responsibility or keep running."

He looked at me in disbelief, then lunged past me, boots clattering on the steps, slapping on the sidewalk as he ran.

I went back inside to clear up my last MacAllister mess.

They nailed him before the end of Main Street.

JACKAL

"Now that's a cruiser," the woman said. Ski looked at the guy and shrugged. A country bar in Regina during Agribition was a bit off his usual territory but the guy looked like any of a hundred guys he'd seen in a dozen bars over the years, a bit of a gut, thinning hair, closer to forty than thirty so he was too old to look like he belonged, too drunk to have more than a sniff at picking up a woman. Not that it seemed to stop them.

"Too deep for me," he said. "Make sense?" he asked Hicks.

"I guess. They cruise the bars trying to pick up anything they can. You gotta admire their persistence."

Hicks' wife, Donna, snorted. "Pathetic is more like it. Bunch of losers who can't find a woman."

Her friend, Bev, who'd started the whole thing, nodded. "Guys like him couldn't handle a relationship if their lives depended on it. They..." Ski tuned her out. It'd just be more of the same man bashing she'd been doing all night. No wonder her old man had left. At least she'd quit getting weepy and whining about her divorce and her ex. That'd made supper a lot of fun. Ski wished Donna's cousin, Susan, had shown up. At least he knew she didn't hate men and he could talk to her almost as easily as he used to talk to Terri.

He took a long pull on his beer and, looking for a likely partner, watched the crowd as the band started a two-step. There was a whole table across the dance floor, including a couple of women in tight jeans who were tottering around on come-fuck-me boots, the whole package just waiting for the right man, the right line. Just what he needed for a night. Just what he needed to forget Terri and all that romantic bullshit. He smiled at the thought of peeling one of the women out of her jeans, her ass lifting off the bed, then the bed-springs creaking as they went at it.

"Anybody ever tell you that your friend is a pig," Bev said to Donna. Ski swung toward her, the smile dropping from his face.

"What the fuck are you talking about?"

"Why don't you just fucking drool when you stare at a woman? You're as bad as the rest of these maggots. Probably figuring out which one of those women would be easiest to get into bed."

"Up yours, lady."

"Easy, Ski," Hicks said. "Jesus, Bev, there's no need for that. Ski never did anything to you."

"He's a man. That's enough." She swayed on the tall stool. "And he's not even good enough to be a cruiser. He's a fucking jackal."

"You don't know what the hell you're talking about." Ski started to stand. "Just because you couldn't keep your old man happy, you're pissed at all of us. Well, tough shit, lady. I'm not gonna be your punching bag just because you're all screwed up."

"Ski – " Donna started as Bev broke into tears. She grabbed her purse, stumbled off toward the bathroom.

"Ski, sometimes you're a real ignorant bastard," Donna said as she got up and followed Bev.

The two men sat in silence for a few moments, Hicks sipping at his beer, Ski taking a large gulp out of his. "What's biting your ass?" Hicks finally asked.

"Nothing. I just didn't feel like taking shit from some broad I don't even know."

"Quit trying to bullshit me. You would've laughed something like that off before. It's Terri's leaving that's bothering you, isn't it?"

"No." Ski picked up Hicks' cigarettes, feeling the craving again after a year. Hicks pulled them out of his hand, dropped them on the table.

"Ski, you've been on edge ever since she left last month. That's why we thought getting away might do you some good, but I'm getting sick of putting up with your moping. Either talk about it or get the hell on with life."

"You wanna know? Fine. She gave me an ultimatum right out of one of those fucking women's magazines. 'Call me when you're ready to make love, not fuck.' What kind of bullshit is that? What the hell is it supposed to mean?"

Hicks looked at Ski and shook his head. "If I've got to explain that, then we're going to be here a while." He waved to get the waitress's attention, then held up his beer bottle and pointed at himself and Ski. She nodded and marked it down. Hicks leaned back in his chair and lit a cigarette. "You've been going out with Terri for how long? Close to a year and a half?"

"Something like that, yeah."

"That's, what, probably a year longer than you ever went out with a woman before."

"Yeah."

"And I know you never cheated on her. Christ, you even quit smoking because of her kid's asthma."

"This isn't about Stephanie, it's about Terri and me."

"OK. Were you happy that year and a half?"

"Yeah." He remembered a hot summer night watching Stephanie ride the pony he'd bought her around the pasture until it was too dark to see, coming in from stabling the horse and washing up as Terri read Stephanie to sleep, then the two of them making love slowly, quietly, in the heat of their bedroom. Or at least that's what he thought they were doing.

"And in all that time you never figured out what she wanted?"

"How the hell are you supposed to figure out what a woman wants? It's not like they're logical or anything. One wants to make love, the next wants to keep things casual or to get something she can't get from her old man."

"You could try listening to what she says. Christ, you expect the answers on a silver platter? Donna and I have been married over ten years and we still mess up on the talking sometimes."

"So what am I supposed to do, ask her to explain things in real small words?"

Hicks laughed. He handed the waitress some money, waved away the change. "It might help." He sipped his beer, leaned forward. "Ski, you know what's going on between you two, I don't, but I bet it wouldn't take much to change."

"What wouldn't take much to change?" Donna asked from behind Ski.

"Nothing," Ski said before Hicks could answer. "Nothing important."

Donna looked at him for a second, then shook her head. "Still doing that macho shit, Ski? I'd hoped you'd finally evolved past that this last year." She held her hand out to her husband. "You mind catching a cab back to the hotel? I'm going to give Bev a ride home and I'll probably be a while."

"No problem." Hicks said, fishing the keys out of his jeans' pocket. "Tell Bev I'm sorry and I'll catch her next time we're in town."

"OK. And keep an eye out for Susan. She might still show up. And try to behave." She looked at Ski. "Both of you."

"We always behave," Hicks said.

"Yeah right. You two get together, have a few drinks, and you develop the worst case of liquor logic I've ever seen."

"We'll be good," Hicks said.

Donna started to turn, then looked at Ski. "Did you wonder what Bev meant when she said you were a jackal, not a cruiser?"

"Jesus, Donna – " Hicks started, before Ski cut him off.

"No and I don't really care."

"Maybe you should. A cruiser, he just bounces around, trying the same old bullshit on every woman he meets until he gets lucky. A jackal, now that's a lot different. He knows exactly what he wants. He picks on the emotional cripples, the ones who've had too much to drink. He knows just what lines to use to appeal to her need for someone who cares, someone who thinks she's special." She stepped up to the table, her back to her husband, her eyes locked on Ski. "They're target practice for him, a convenient place to stick his dick. Was that what the women before Terri were, Ski? Convenient holes."

"That's enough!" Hicks put his hand on his wife's arm. "Ski's our friend, for Christ sake, not some low-life bar scum."

"Isn't he?" She shook his hand off. "Ski, I've always stuck up for you, but I see so much that sounds just like the guys who've been preying on Bev that I don't know if I can ever look at you the same way again."

"Fine. Look at me any way you fucking well want. You've already convicted me so why should I even bother saying anything? Just answer me one question. Have you ever seen me hunting hurting women? Huh? Have you?"

She smiled sadly. "How good were that Waller girl or Jan Wozniak feeling when you slept with them?" Ski stayed silent. "I thought so," she said. "Good night, Ski. See if you can find something to keep you warm." She turned and walked away.

Ski silently watched her leave, his hands clenched around his beer bottle. He didn't hear Hicks' next question and barely noticed him shrugging and waving at the shooter waitress. He also barely noticed the waitress as she placed a shot of tequila in front of him. Donna's words burned at him. Sharon Waller, Jan Wozniak. He hadn't thought of them in a long time. Sure they were drunk when he'd slept with them, but he hadn't poured the booze into them. So Sharon had just broke up with her old man and Jan was down about losing her job and not being married at thirty. So what, they were both adults, both willing. He hadn't gone after them because they were hurting; he'd gone after them because they were good-looking and ready for a wild night out. Besides, they hadn't been hurting that bad, had they? Shit. He picked up the tequila, slammed it back, not bothering with the salt and lime. He shook his head as the liquor burned its way down, sipped his beer to cool the fire.

"She's wrong, you know. They both knew what they were doing. It's not like she said." He looked at Hicks, waiting, hoping, for his support.

"Hey, I'm on your side. If they were fucked up, it's not your fault. You're not responsible for what they do."

"Exactly." Ski waved the shooter waitress over again. "Two tequila, *por favor.*" He smiled at her. She flashed her teeth quickly and set the drinks on the table. Ski looked her over as he fished his wallet out. Tall brunette, cowboy hat sitting on top of brown curls. Not as much up front as he liked, not like Terri, but what there was was high and firm and he knew from watching her before that the ass was prime under the skin-tight jeans. He knew better than to hit on her though. It was almost impossible to get anywhere with waitresses. Better to try the table across the dance floor.

"To us," he said, raising his glass high. "Free in the city, no women, no cares." He fired back the shooter. "That's more like it. All that stuff about evolving and cruisers and jackals is bullshit. Fucking women think too much."

"Yeah, but every once in a while they get it right."

"You don't mean – "

"No, not you. I was thinking of Koenig."

"That maggot! What's he got to do with this?"

"Think about it. The way he almost raped Brenda after she split up with her old man. Or the time at that ball dance when he got that drunk blonde from Prince Albert into his truck." Hicks' knuckles were white around his beer bottle. "Never thought I'd be glad to see MacAllister kick the shit out of someone."

"That's different. He wasn't smooth or smart or anything. He was just a fucking low-life who sometimes fooled really drunk women."

"Maybe, but how'd he talk them into going with him? And quite a few didn't scream."

"Anybody can do that."

"Really?"

"OK, so I'm a little smoother than most guys. More *evolved*," he said, stressing the last word. And he wasn't like any of those guys Bev had been talking about. They were so obvious. Dressed to impress. He kept it simple, a denim shirt, faded jeans, and well-broken-in cowboy boots. Just a guy out for a beer. And if the woman was interested, great. If not, there was always someone else. No need to take it personally. He smiled and drained his beer. "I think I know just how to show how smooth I am," he said, picking up another beer from the table. "Wish me luck." He walked around the dance floor, a smile on his face, lines running through his head. Lines? Shit. This was different. Every guy used a line to start the talking. Every guy. A couple of the women were smiling as they saw him coming, but others were watching him with careful eyes. Too bad. The group looked large enough that they wouldn't all be close, wouldn't all be trying to look out for the others, not like when there were four or less.

"Hi, I'm Ski. I saw you ladies here and just had to come over and talk to you."

"Gee, aren't we blessed," one of the watchful ones said. Ski could see the ring on her left hand. Married women! What a pain in the ass. Figured just because they weren't having any fun that none of their single friends should. Ski gave her his best aw-shucks-farm-boy grin.

"I guess that sounded like a line. Sorry, it's just me and my buddy are down for Agribition and I thought it'd be nice to talk to some pretty women." He waved his hand toward where Hicks sat. "My buddy, he's okay to talk to, but he sure isn't anything to look at." Ski stood. "But if I'm bothering you, I guess he'll have to do."

"Sit down," one of the smiling ones said. No ring and a blouse undone far enough to show lots of white skin and cleavage. Bingo. "Quit being such a tight-ass, Linda, he's just being friendly."

"Whatever," Linda said, looking at Ski and shaking her head. She picked up her drink. "I'm going to talk to Dianne. Have fun." She walked to the far end of the table and started talking to another woman with an even bigger rock on her ring finger. They both looked at Ski as he leaned on the table and turned his back to them. The woman sat on a tall stool, her eyes level with Ski's. He gave her his best smile as he checked her out. She was young, maybe twenty-one or twenty-two, dirty blonde hair, on the short side, starting to pudge out a bit, but with breasts just the way he liked them, large and firm under the white frilly blouse. Built for comfort, not speed, as the old saying went, but Ski thought she'd have a lot of speed to her. The comfort was a bonus.

"Thanks. Your friend doesn't seem to like me."

"Ignore her. A friend of ours had a bad experience with a guy she met in here and now Linda figures she has to protect us all. You don't look that dangerous to me though." She held out her hand. "I'm Jody."

Ski took the soft hand, shook it, held it a moment longer than necessary. "Pleased to meet you, Jody. And I'm glad you think I'm not dangerous."

"I didn't say you don't look dangerous. Just not *that* dangerous." She smiled hesitantly at him, looking for approval of the soap opera dialogue, trying to look older and more confident than her voice sounded. "And maybe danger is just what I need tonight."

Ski struggled to keep the smile off his face. Nailed it on the first try. Eighteen months hadn't slowed him down. He had to take it easy though, or her friends would get in the way. Convince her that he was interested in more than sex even though she seemed to know the score. Donna and her crap about vulnerable women. This one knew what she wanted. Shit, he'd take her for breakfast with Greg and Donna. He'd show Donna *evolved*.

"Well, maybe I'll get dangerous later, but right now you look like you need a dance."

She looked at the dance floor, listened for a second. "I'm not really that good at the two-step."

"Nothing to it. I'll lead. Come on." He took her hand and led her to the crowded dance floor. She slid hesitantly into his arms and he smiled at her again. "Relax," he said as they started shuffling in time to the music, unable to move freely on the postcard-sized dance floor with its dozens of couples. Ski worked her over to the side away from her friends. He grunted as another couple bounced off him and pulled her closer to stop her from getting stepped into. She didn't pull back and Ski could feel the heat of her body, her breasts against him. It had been too long. The song ended and she stayed close.

"One more?" he asked.

"Sure, unless – Sorry I'm not really ready for a slow song." She pulled back slightly and he let her go.

"No problem." They threaded their way through the couples clinging tightly to each other, Ski's hand resting lightly in the small of her back. He saw Hicks watching him and winked at him over her head. Hicks shook his head and raised his beer bottle in salute. Ski looked quickly at the women's table but none of them seemed to have noticed the exchange. They sat on the high stools and sipped at their drinks. He had to regain his momentum.

"So what do you do when you're not here?" he asked and tried not to wince. Maybe the long break had been harder than he thought.

"I'm a waitress at a Greek place downtown..." She started in about her job and Ski nodded and laughed in the right places, asking questions when she slowed down, buying her a drink when the waitress came around, giving her bits and pieces of his own life whenever she asked a question. He found himself relaxing, the laughter becoming real, unforced as they talked about her strange customers, his crazy horses, and the wild times they'd had at ball tournaments. She was a fun kid, happy and able to take pleasure in the simple things in life. And innocent, Ski thought. Somehow the thought didn't excite him like it used to. Instead it depressed him. He was too used to Terri, to her keen eye, her biting sense of humour, her independence. This kid was just trying to play the role of independent woman. And failing. Damn Donna and her theories, but he had to know.

"Not that I'm complaining, but finding somebody as pretty as you without a boyfriend is rare. How'd I get so lucky?"

She flushed and took a quick sip of her drink. "I guess you could say I'm between boyfriends." She kept her eyes lowered and stirred her drink.

Shit. Leave it alone. You don't want to know the answer. But the word jackal kept running through his head. "What – "

"Bathroom break?" It was Linda.

"Sure." Jody got off her stool and picked up her purse. "I'll be right back. Don't go away."

"Sure." He watched her walk away, a frown on his face. What didn't she want him to know? He took a pull on his beer. And why the hell should he care? Donna. Fuck. Even having women as friends messed with your mind. He turned and looked down the table. Most of the women were up dancing, but the older married woman Linda was talking to earlier was still there. He grabbed his beer and walked down to her.

"Hi." he said as he sat down across from her. "I'm Ski."

"Dianne."

"Friend of Jody's?"

"We play slow-pitch on the same team."

"She's a nice kid."

"Yeah, she is and she doesn't need any more shit in her life right now."

"And you figure I'd raise shit in her life?"

"She's young, she's rebounding and she still figures she can meet Mr. Right in a bar." She looked at him, shook her head. "No offence, but you look like you've been around awhile, so you know that it just doesn't happen."

"No, not often." Except that he'd met Terri in a bar and they'd been happy. Could be happy. "What's she rebounding from?" Damn Donna to Hell.

"What do you care?"

"Like I said, she's a nice kid." He started to give her one of his aw shucks looks, then stopped. "Maybe I just don't want to hurt her."

"Yeah right." She studied his face. He couldn't tell what she found there, but her eyes narrowed in thought for a second and then she shrugged. "No big secret. It's from her high school sweetheart. Only guy she ever really went out with. He went off to school in Calgary and ended up boffing some nursing student. Poor kid just about died when she found out." She looked Ski in the eye. "Now she wants to be badder than she is, to do all the things she figures her ex was looking for, but she's really a good kid." She smiled wryly. "Linda's in there right now telling her that you'd be bad for her."

"And she's probably right." Shit, what was this? A year and a half and he'd turned into a fucking boy scout? The word whispered in his head again. Jackal. He bit his lip, then nodded. "Look, tell her I had to talk to my buddy. I'll get him to pull us out of here and she gets a soft fall."

She frowned. "Sure, but...I guess Linda and I were wrong about you."

"Maybe." He stood and picked up his beer. "Tell her what I said. I'll stop by on the way out and get Hicks to play the asshole."

"Sure. And thanks."

"Yeah." He started to turn, then stopped as she put her hand on his arm. He looked at her curiously.

"One good turn deserves another," she said. She pointed to the dance floor. "See the guy in black?"

"Which one?" There had to be half a dozen Johnny Cash wannabees on the dance floor.

"The one with the woman I saw talking to your buddy a little while ago." She shook her head as he scanned the dance floor blankly for several seconds and said, "The one with the bottle blonde with the overdeveloped chest."

Okay, that he could follow. He picked them out, then frowned. The woman looked familiar... Oh shit. Donna's cousin, Susan. Hair was a different colour and she'd lost some weight. It was definitely her, but it was the guy who made the hair on his neck stand up. Everything was in place, the whole urban cowboy thing, big hat, shirt done up to the neck, a belt buckle the size of a hubcap, boots that had never seen shit. Asshole probably even had a duster in the coat check. And never rode a horse in his life.

"Your buddy's friend will be lucky if she can walk straight tomorrow," Dianne said.

Shit. Was nothing going to go right tonight? "What do you mean by that?"

"The bastard picked up a friend of ours a couple of weeks ago," she said. "She was pretty drunk and feeling down because she kept on meeting jerks and losers, then along comes Mr. Sympathy and she's got somebody who understands her." She pulled a cigarette from her pack and lit it, her movements jerky. "Motherfucker poured drinks into her all evening, then talked her into taking him home." She shook her head, mashed the cigarette into the ashtray. "Mr. Nice Guy barely made it through the front door."

"He raped her?"

"Yes. No. Oh, I don't know what the fuck you call it. She was ready to get laid but not like that. Not rough and mean like that. She was sore for days. And I don't know what all happened but she still doesn't want to go out. Cried for a couple of days. Still does once in a while."

A smoother Koenig, a jackal, Ski thought. He watched the guy whisper in Susan's ear as their bodies swayed in rythym, tight together. Looked like she was his target tonight.

"She a friend of yours?" Dianne asked. She had another cigarette going and Ski stepped back to avoid the smoke.

"No, just my buddy's wife's cousin that I met a couple of times," Ski said, hoping to keep her talking.

"Yeah? Well she could be just right for him. She's been going crazy the last couple of months."

"What do you mean?" Ski said.

"She's been in here a lot in the last six months, doing what Jody thinks she could."

"Huh?" He wondered if the beer was getting to him.

"She's been sleeping around a lot. Linda's sister went to school with her. Guess she's split up with her husband and is going through a messy divorce. Going to kill herself if she isn't careful."

Shit! He had to tell Hicks, get him to do something, because he'd done his good deed for the day and wasn't that all a boy scout had to do? He spotted Jody and Linda leaving the bathroom. "Time to go," he said. Dianne followed his glance and nodded.

"I'll give her the story."

"Good." Ski hurried back to where Hicks sat watching him. "Sorry. Thought I had me something there. Guess I was wrong."

"Didn't look like you were wrong." Hicks frowned at him. "What's up? It's not like you to give up that easily. Still thinking of Terri?"

"Drop it, OK." Ski drained his beer. "It wasn't Terri. This place is just getting to me and that mess with Donna and her weird friend left a shitty taste in my mouth. But we've got something more important to worry about."

"Which is?"

"I saw Susan – "

"Yeah, she stopped by and said hello. She really wanted to talk to you but she saw you with the little blonde and said maybe some other time." He frowned as he looked at the dance floor. "Looks like she found somebody else already. Guess you're out of luck."

Shit, shit, shit. Ski ran a hand over his face. What the hell else was going to happen tonight? Maybe he should just forget it. Not even tell Greg. No, they'd always been straight with each other. "Uh, Greg, we've got a problem."

"Yeah? What?"

"The guy's another Koenig. If you let her leave with him, she's going to be walking bowlegged tomorrow." He paused. "If she's lucky."

"Fuck. You sure?"

"Yep. She likely to listen if you tell her what's what?"

"Not tonight. She's pissed and in a strange mood. Never seen her like this before. Course the breakup and her big-mouthed, asshole ex-husband screwed her up pretty bad." Hicks drummed his fingers on the table. "Can't leave her with him. Donna would kill us. Ski, you gotta take her away from him."

"What? Where'd you get that genius idea? Donna's already not speaking to me. If I pick up her cousin, she'll never talk to me again. I'll be lucky if she lets me into the yard, let alone the house."

"I'll take care of that. Look, it sounded like Susan really remembered that night you spent together at the lake. You're in if you give it a shot. Besides, I didn't say you had to sleep with her, just get her away. Take her home, then bail out. That'll give me a chance to talk to her tomorrow when her head is on straighter. I'll warn her about the asshole."

Ski shook his head. He needed a smoke. And to get the hell away from this city. It was too fucking strange for him. He lifted his beer bottle. Empty. Great. He looked around. No waitress. Shit. He watched the fake cowboy guide Susan around the dance floor, hand firm on her back, lips close to her ear as he shouted over the music. She laughed. He smiled, sharp and sharklike.

"Shit, anything to cut that asshole off at the knees." He just hoped he could get free without a big scene. He looked up at where Jody was talking to her friends. There was another problem. What was she going to think when she saw him with another woman? He hoped Dianne would take care of it.

He shook his head. If this was what evolving meant, then evolution sucked.

"When did life get so complicated?" he asked Hicks.

"It always has been," Hicks replied. "You just finally grew up enough to notice."

"Great." Terri, Donna, Jody, and now Susan, it was all too much. Ten years since he'd boinked her in his tent and now he was getting in shit for it? Bullshit. "Isn't there another way to do this?"

"You got any better ideas?"

"You sure you can't just talk to her?"

"I told you, she's in a strange mood," Hicks said. "She might just go with the asshole to show me I'm wrong. So, either you pick her up, or you pull a MacAllister and kick the shit out of the guy."

Hmmm. The guy was Ski's height, but on the skinny side. Ski figured he had forty pounds on the guy. Wouldn't be much of a fight. He shook his head. He knew better. Solving problems by fighting was Mac's thing, not his. No, Greg's solution was the only one that came to mind.

Ski sat lost in thought as Hicks ordered them more beer. Was all this going on around him before and he hadn't noticed? He knew he'd tried to listen more when he was with Terri, but even though he heard the words, the meaning always seemed to be just out of his reach. Make love, not fuck. Later. He had to get out of this first.

"What if I can't get away from her? I sleep with her and Donna'll kill us both. We've got to think of something else."

"Such as? Look, Ski, I know what Donna said is bugging you, but this is different. You're helping her." Hicks paused as the waitress set down the beer, paid her, waved away the change. "Besides, getting away is easy. Pour the drinks and make hers really stiff. Yap a bit and she'll be out like a light. Toss a blanket over her and away you go. It's not rocket science."

Ski stared at Hicks in disbelief. "Where'd you learn shit like that?"

"Darchuk told me about doing it once." Hicks smiled. "Nice to know one boy scout."

"Two, if Terri and Donna get their way."

"Would that be so bad?" Hicks waved toward where Susan and the imitation cowboy sat on the other side of the dance floor. "You want to end up like that? Hasn't been another guy as much as say hi to him all night. He laughs and smiles but look at his eyes."

Ski looked and nodded. "Never makes it to the eyes." He felt himself go cold.

"Yeah," Hicks continued, not noticing Ski's stricken look. "Reminds me of a weasel I cornered by the barn one time."

"Or the Vulture," Ski said softly.

"The Vulture..." Hicks shook himself. "Ski, you've done some scary things to get laid, but that took the cake."

"No shit." Five years gone by and it was like yesterday. Older than him, but a hard body still and a looker. Classy. He'd been unable to believe his luck and too stupid to see she was using him. What did he care, he was getting laid. So she was distant, so she said things in public that cut him down, so she'd been bossy in bed, so his friends didn't like her, so what? He was getting fucked silly. Any time, any position. He'd been as happy as a pig in shit until the night they did it with the lights on. He'd looked down into her eyes and they'd been hard, measuring, judging him, his performance. No emotion, no feeling for him, just calculation. He'd never felt so unimportant, so cold and empty inside. He'd finished quickly, before she came, and left, her profanity and laughter following him. It'd been a couple of months before he tried to pick up a woman again and he'd picked up a young one then.

Damn. He thought he'd buried all that. Seemed like this was the night for his whole past to come back to haunt him. He looked at Susan and the jackal again, thought about the night he had spent with her at the lake, undressing her in his cramped pup tent, her silence at first, then the wildest ride he'd had up until then, her fingernails digging into his back, her hips thrusting against him, her gasping and screaming. He'd felt like he'd fallen into a porn movie. Ten years and he still remembered the music from the party a couple of campsites over, the sweat gleaming on her skin in the heat of the tent, and the quiet talk as they curled up together on the sleeping bag afterwards. He also remembered running into her at Hicks' over the years since then, the flirting when her husband wasn't around, the looks the guy gave him. Then meeting her six months ago at Greg and Donna's, her quietness during the barbecue and Terri saying while they were driving home, "She's a hurting woman." Damn. She didn't need to think of this asshole in five years. Nobody needed to feel like he did with the Vulture.

"OK, Hicks, I'll do it. Just keep Donna off of me."

"No problem. If I got to I'll tell her it was my idea and take the shit for it." He sighed. "Don't fuck up though. Get her home and pull a Darchuk or we're both dead."

"Yeah, I know." He got up, stretched. "Wish me luck. Again." He walked away, rolling his shoulders to get the kinks out. He stopped at the bar and got a beer and a couple of China Whites. Women always liked the smoother shooters and it'd make escaping a bit easier. He looked up and saw her watching him. He smiled and weaved through the crowd to where she and the jackal stood by the stand-up bar against the wall.

"Hi, Susan, it's been a long time." He handed her the drink. "Thought we'd celebrate both of us being free."

"I'd like that, Ski." She took the drink, raised it to him. They clinked glasses and fired the shooters back in one gulp. She licked her lips and smiled. "I love China Whites." She frowned briefly as the jackal cleared his throat. "Ski, this is Derek. Derek, this is Ski, an old friend of mine. We partied together before I was married."

"Ski," Derek said, his eyes hard, watchful, his tone cool.

"Pleased to meet you, Derek," Ski said, giving the jackal his best goofy smile and holding out his hand. The jackal took it and squeezed hard. Ski kept the smile on his face and squeezed back, overcoming the pressure and watching the jackal's face tighten. He kept the pressure on for a second, letting the jackal know he was out of his league if he tried to get physical, then released his hand with a laugh.

"That's some grip you've got there, Derek. You work out?"

"Yeah," the jackal said, frowning.

"Thought so," Ski said, smiling even wider. "You know this really is a small city. I actually met some people who know you." He pointed to the table where Jody and her friends sat. "You know one of their friends, right?"

The jackal took a quick look. His lips thinned and he stared icily at Ski. Ski met his stare, letting the smile drop. "You do remember their friend, don't you, because she really remembers you."

"I know a lot of people."

"You want me to remind you how you know her?"

"No, I remember now." His body was tight and Ski measured the distance between them. Too far for a sucker punch and he was close enough to step into a kick. Time to end it.

"You don't mind if I dance with Susan do you? Guy like you should be able to find a dancing partner easy enough."

"No problem." He stepped back, still glaring at Ski.

Ski smirked at him and stepped beside Susan. "Ready to dance, pretty lady?"

"Uh, sure," she said, looking blearily from one of them to the other. "You sure it's okay, Derek?"

"It's fine."

"Of course it's fine. Derek's a good sport; aren't you, Derek?"

The jackal's face flushed and his voice was tight. "Get fucked."

"Not likely," Ski said, putting his arm around Susan, "at least for you."

The jackal's fists clenched at his side.

Ski felt Susan sway against him and took a quick glance at her. She was frowning at him, but seemed content to see what was going to happen.

Ski held the jackal's eyes until the smaller man looked away.

"So dance together," the jackal said, smirking at Ski. "Susan and I can always get together some other time."

"I'd like that," Susan said.

"You will," the jackal said, then turned and disappeared into the crowd on the dance floor.

Ski looked down at Susan. She was looking up at him, a hesitant expression on her face. He grinned at her. "I'd like to catch up. How about we grab another drink and talk?"

"I was thinking we should go somewhere more private, like my place."

Ski kept the grimace on his face. No way to avoid it, he was going to have to pull a Darchuk. Two good deeds in one night. Was that worth something or would Donna still think he was some sort of unevolved lowlife? Donna. Had to make one more try because you never knew what might happen at Susan's place.

"Your place? Sounds good, but, uh, what about Donna?"

"What about Donna? None of her business what we do."

"Yeah, I know, but with Hicks here..."

"Greg didn't care last time we got together so why should he now?"

"Ya, why should he?" Ski followed her as she pulled him toward Hicks' table. He didn't like the sound of "last time we got together." And last time Hicks and Donna were still newly married, without kids and in party mode. They'd changed. So had she. So had he. At least he knew none of this would get back to Terri through Hicks. If only he was as sure about Donna.

"Greg, Ski is going to drive me home. I've had a bit too much to drink."

Hicks smiled at her. "Sure. Got cab fare, Ski?"

"I'm fine." He looked at Hicks from behind Susan and raised his shoulders in a slight shrug. "I'll see you at the fairgrounds in the morning."

"Sure thing. And I'll say hello to Darchuk for you."

"Yeah, tell him I owe him one." Ski set his almost full beer on the table. "Let's go," he said, guiding Susan toward the door. They stopped at the coat check and Ski looked back into the bar toward Jody. She was watching him, her face set and angry, shaking her head as Dianne spoke to her. Linda sat next to her smiling contentedly. Finally Dianne looked up, shrugged toward Ski and mouthed the word "sorry." He nodded and felt a sad smile flit across his face. Who'd've thought he could leave a horny woman pissed off at him and think it for the best? He shook his head as he followed Susan out to the parking lot.

"Where to," he said as he started the car.

"I'll show you, but first – " She leaned over and kissed him, her lips hard on his, her mouth open and ready. He hesitated, then returned the kiss. It went on for a long time, then he pulled back.

"Let's get to your place," he said, his breath coming sharp and ragged.

She grinned, a slow sleepy smile. "Yeah, let's." She slid up against the console, leaned against him and dropped her hand to his thigh. "Hurry."

He drove slowly, carefully, aware of her insistent hand on his leg, her breasts against his arm. Hicks owed him big time. All too soon they were pulling into the parking lot behind her building.

"Home, sweet home," she said, kissing him quickly. They slid out of the car and she came up against him, her arm around him, her hand in his back pocket. He put his arm around her too and they walked inside, hips bumping each other and him guiding her when she stumbled.

The apartment was small, a single bedroom right off the hallway when they came in. A double bed was pushed into the corner, two teddy bears sitting on a white bedspread. She pulled him toward it.

"Let's have a drink first," he said, dragging his heels. "It'll be better if we take our time."

She looked at him, unsure. "You're not trying to back out on me, are you? Scared of Donna?"

"To hell with Donna," he said, kissing her hard. She moaned and slid into him, her arms tight around him. He could taste the whisky, the cigarettes, the shooters. Finally he pulled away. "Slowly. It's better that way. Trust me."

"Okay, but I don't remember you being this slow before."

"I've learned some new tricks over the years," he said, leering at her.

She smiled. "Good. So have I." She turned and walked to the bathroom. "Booze is under the sink, mix in the fridge."

"Great," he said, as she closed the door behind her.

"Fuck," he said under his breath. This wasn't working like it should. She wasn't as drunk as she should be. And too fucking horny. He took out the rye and poured her glass half full. He made his a single, then put a big splash into it. His hands shook slightly. This was wrong. This should be Terri. This should be simple. He'd been here enough times before; why should it be any different now?

He took the drinks into the darkened living room, sank onto the couch and took a large gulp. Darchuk had better have been right. He had no idea what to do if she didn't pass out. He frowned as he heard the shower running. What the hell was she doing? He looked at the door. Grab his boots and run? Who gave a shit what she thought. Or he could just sleep with her. It'd be a wild ride and there was no reason he shouldn't. Except for Terri. And Donna. What a mess. Grown up enough to notice how complicated things were, Hicks had said. Great. It was easier being an overaged kid, unevolved. Like those guys close to forty who were still cruising the bars, still not noticing anything around them. Did he want to end up like that? No fucking way. Bunch of losers. Bev had been right about that. He looked at the door again. So tempting, but was it fair to her? Wasn't hurting Bev, Donna, and Jody enough for one evening? He sighed, drank again. He found himself smirking. Enough to drink and he'd be the one to pass out. Or could he fake it? Darchuk probably would. Maybe –

The door to the bathroom swung open, the light silhouetting her. He squinted, then froze. All she was wearing was a short kimono-style robe. She smiled at him and walked to the couch, sinking down beside him, the robe riding up until it was barely covering her crotch, gaping open to show most of her breasts. Ski looked and felt a twinge of desire, remembering her fingernails on his back, her breath on his neck. She picked up her drink, took a sip.

"Sorry I took so long but I was fading so I took a shower to wake up. Now where were we?" She put her drink down, slid next to him and kissed him, her finger working at the buttons on his shirt. Her breath tasted of spearmint. Her hands slid inside his shirt and tugged it from his pants, then started unbuckling his belt.

"Lift up," she said, as she broke the kiss. Instead he pulled back.

"I can't do this to Terri. I thought I could, but I was wrong."

She looked at him, confusion on her face. "What the hell was all that in the bar then? You like playing games with people?" Her robe had fallen completely open and Ski found himself staring at her breasts. So beautiful; so wrong. Despite everything though, he felt himself hardening.

"No, it's just she's special..."

"And I'm just somebody you don't even want to sleep with. Thanks a lot." She pulled the robe together and sniffled. Not tears, he thought. Get mad, scream, I can deal with that, but not tears. Please not tears.

"No, it's not like that. You're beautiful, just like you were ten years ago. And I still remember that night in the tent, but things are different now."

"Quit bullshitting me. You don't think I'm beautiful.

You just want to be able to tell yourself what a nice guy you are, letting me down gently after you lost your nerve." She wiped her hand across her nose. "At least Derek wanted to make love to me."

Shit, shit, shit. This wasn't working the way it was supposed to. Even if she listened to Hicks about the jackal tomorrow, she'd still probably end up with somebody at least as bad next weekend. She deserved better. She deserved someone who would at least try to make love to her, not just fuck her.

He put a hand under her chin, lifted her head so she could see his eyes. "I'm not bullshitting you." He kissed her gently, then with more force. She resisted momentarily, then her mouth opened. The robe fell open and he caressed her breast. She sighed.

"Please," she said. He nodded. Wordlessly they got up and went into the bedroom.

She shrugged the robe off when they got to the bed and started to tug at his belt again. He took her hands in his and pulled her to him. They kissed for a long time, sinking slowly to the bed. He pulled back as she finished unbuttoning his shirt, yanked it over his head. The rest of his clothes quickly followed it to the floor. She pulled at him and all the moves from the tent were there again, the hip thrusts, the moaning. Ski touched her cheek softly.

"Shh." He kissed her, quieting the exaggerated moans, part of the act. He stroked her breasts, kissed her neck, slowly working his way down her body for long delicious minute after long delicious minute until the moans became more subdued, became genuine. Only then did he move between her legs.

She gasped at the first touch of his tongue, her fingers digging into his hair, her legs spreading open. He teased her with his tongue, his fingers, doing all the things he'd learned Terri loved so well, building the tempo until she thrust her hips into his face. He rode her out, tonguing her until she slumped back onto the bed.

He slid up the bed and they kissed. Her breathing started to slow and he began caressing her again. She wrapped her hand around him, kissed his chest and began sliding down the bed. He stopped her, not wanting her to lose her edge.

"This is your night," he said as he moved between her legs again. She held him as he slid into her, and they made love, her hand between them. There were none of the acrobatics from the tent, none of the different positions, just the two of them face to face, settling into a steady rhythm, mouths busy.

Later, as they lay spent, curled up like spoons, she pulled his arm across her and snuggled against his chest, sighing contentedly. He stared off into space, hating himself, realizing what Terri meant, finally understanding all the emotions he'd never noticed before, the feelings that could turn sex into making love, the giving without expecting something in return. And the sadness, the bittersweet pleasure that could be there, had been there before.

CONTROL

You wouldn't think a family supper would be the type of thing that would give a guy butterflies before he got there, would you? In the Brant household we did things differently of course. It wasn't the food that gave us indigestion, it was each other. Or rather my Dad and me. Mom just tried to keep the conversation going and tried to keep us from blowing up at each other. Lately, she'd been fairly successful, mainly because I was tired of fighting with the old man. No, I'd been ramming my head against that particular wall for way too long. This would be my last attempt to talk some sense into him. If it didn't work tonight, then I'd had enough of his bullshit, his controlling ways, his refusal to treat me like a partner in the farm, like a man. I'd worked up to this over the last year and a half, and a week ago on New Year's Eve I decided it was time to finally confront him.

Still, that could wait until after dessert. We could glare and grunt at each other until then, each pretending that he didn't think the other was the biggest fuck-up to ever come out of Pine Valley.

"One scoop or two, Ken?" Mom asked me as she shoved the big spoon into the ice cream pail.

I looked at the size of the piece of pie she'd cut and smothered a grin. She was still trying to calm me down by spoiling me with dessert. The slice she'd served me was big enough to turn a tractor around on.

"Two," I said, smiling. "I don't think one would even begin to cover that humungous slab."

"It's not that big," she said. She smiled a bit herself and I felt a pang of guilt. When Dad and I locked horns it was always Mom who took it hardest. She was in the middle and tried to peacekeep, but it was a wasted effort. Dad had his ideas about how things were done and how things were going to go in the future, and they just wouldn't change. I'd tried and she'd tried to help me, but it always came down to "My farm, my rules." Okay, if that was the way he wanted to play it, then that's the way we'd play it. Only this time I had a few cards up my sleeve and I was ready to use them.

"Big enough," I said as I took the pie from her. "You spoil me. And," I patted my stomach, "you're making my baby grow."

"You need to get off your ass and do more work then," Dad said. I bit my lip. Not yet. I'd promised Mom I wouldn't argue with him during supper and I meant to keep my word.

No matter how hard it was.

"Edward! There's no need to be like that." Mom

frowned at Dad, her lips a tight line. It rolled off him like water off a duck's back.

"It's my house. I'll say what I want." He quit glaring at me and looked at her. "Am I getting my pie or what?"

"Get it yourself." Mom shoved the ice cream pail toward him and dropped down onto her chair. "It doesn't cost anything to be polite you know."

The old man just grunted and stretched his arm out to snag his pie from in front of Mom. As he slopped a big pile of ice cream onto it, I smothered a snide remark. I might've put on ten pounds in the last couple of years, but the old man had been piling it on for years. The farther his hairline went back, the farther his gut went out. He dealt with both things the same way: denial. He covered the bald spot with a few strands of hair combed over from the side and cemented into place with Brylcreem, and wore suspenders so he could undo his pants when he thought no one was looking. He tried saying he wore the same size pants as when he was married. He never mentioned the gut that hung over those same size pants. I was tempted to say something, but I fought the urge. Getting smart-ass now would make things explode big time. Five minutes to finish dessert and then Dad and I could go outside for a smoke and have it out.

A fun five minutes it wasn't going to be. The tension was so thick that trying to cut it with a knife would just shatter the blade. No, this was chainsaw tension and it was the tension that had built up between Dad and me ever since I'd taken an off-farm job. That, he might have been able to put up with it if was just for the cash, but

I'd actually looked for a job I'd like and found one. A woodworking job. Not only did I like it, but I was damn good at it. For most fathers that would be a reason to be happy, right? Not for mine. I was being irresponsible, I was ignoring the farm, I was putting all he and my grandfather had worked for in jeopardy. Like it was my problem that Grandpa had lost a farm down on the prairies when Dad was a kid in the thirties. Like it was my problem that they'd had to move north to Pine Valley and that getting back to where he'd been financially became Grandpa's Holy Grail. Like it was my problem that Dad had taken up where Grandpa had left off. That was what they'd chosen for their lives. I had to live my life for me and not for the farm. I wanted to control my life, not have the farm control me.

That was the real problem, control. To say that Dad was a control freak was the understatement of all understatements. There were two ways to do things on the farm, his way and the wrong way. And even if he was wrong, he'd never admit it. I just couldn't do anything right. Supposedly I'd screw up something as simple as making chop. It wasn't rocket science, but I always seemed to get the mix wrong, or grind it too fine. Or too coarse. And it didn't matter if I changed next time to what he'd said. No, then I was wrong all over again. And that was just one small example. If I wanted to plant wheat, he wanted canola. If I thought it was too windy to spray, he thought it was fine. If I thought a cow needed a Caesarean, he'd say wait. And, of course, the opposite was true. I couldn't get it right, couldn't win. It made me wonder why I'd taken so long to give up fighting. Too stubborn I guess. That was one way we were alike.

I took a big bite of pie. Apple. My favourite. And Mom had made roast beef. Dad's favourite. It was a good try on Mom's part, but it'd take a lot more than food to mellow Dad and me.

On the plus side, this was the last time she'd have to listen to us. We'd settle things one way or another tonight.

"That was good," the old man said, shoving himself back from the table. "I've got that cow to check on." He glared at me for no particular reason that I could see. I met his gaze silently. I'd had girlfriends who raved over how blue his eyes were. Sky blue, one had said. Maybe, but when he looked at me, it was the sky when it was forty below outside. The only time I saw warmth in them was when he was angry. Made me glad I'd inherited Mom's eyes. They were green. A warm green. I didn't say anything when the old man finally turned away, just watched him stomp out of the room.

"I see the bug up his ass hasn't shrunk any," I said.

"Ken, he's trying. It's just..."

"Just?" I raised an eyebrow at Mom. "Just what? Explain to me why he's the way he is. Why can't he let me try anything new? He just wants to do more of the same."

That was the core of most of my arguments with dad over the years. There weren't a lot of ways to go in farming now. You could either get bigger and more efficient or you could specialize. Dad was old school, so he thought more land was always better. The more efficient part of it seemed to escape him though. And specialization, which I favoured, was just a bunch of "fads."

"Your dad is too old to learn new tricks. He's trying to do his best with what he knows."

"But he doesn't know jack squat."

"Ken – "

I waved her objection away. "Sorry, but it gets so frustrating. Buying a whole bunch of land just means more debt unless you use it properly."

"I don't know about all that. I just know that he wants to leave you a farm that you can make a living with."

"So he's doing all this for me?" I laughed. "That'd be a lot more believable if he ever worked with me now to get my farm so I can make a real living off it. I'm just a hired hand on his farm, with a hobby farm of my own. If I'm going to live like that, isn't it better I work at a job that pays half-decently and where they treat me with a little respect?" My voice had risen at the end of the speech and I took several deep breaths.

Mom looked at me anxiously. A short, plump, blonde woman, her yellowed fingers and coffee-stained teeth betrayed her two vices.

"I know it seems like he never listens," she said, "but he means well."

I snorted. "You could talk until you were blue in the face and never convince me of that," I said. I finished the last of my pie and drained my glass of milk. For a second I felt twelve years old again. Then I remembered the old man waiting out at the barn. That was one thing I'd say for the miserable old bastard, he was good about taking it outside. He didn't want to hurt Mom any more than I did. No, we could scream at each other in the barnyard or in a field to our heart's content, but the house was off limits. Worked for me, even if it took a lot of self-control sometimes.

I stood up and started gathering dishes.

"I can do that," Mom said.

"It's not a problem," I said. And it wasn't. But I was just procrastinating and I knew it. I was about to take a big step, a likely irreversible step, and that scared me. We quickly got all the dishes into the sink though and it was time to take the bull by the horns. Or kick the bull in the ass, or whatever it was I was doing.

"Thanks for supper," I said, taking my cap from the hook by the door.

"You're not coming back in?" Mom was twisting a dishtowel in her hands, hands squeezed tight.

I shook my head. "You know what's going to happen when I go out there. By the time we're done, I won't want to be around him any more than he'll want to be around me."

"Can't you try to keep the conversation civil?" The towel was a tight braid now, her knuckles white.

"That's never worked before, why should it now?" I tried a smile. "Don't worry. No matter what's said, you're still welcome at my place any time. This is between me and him."

"Is that supposed to make me feel better? I can't stand to see you two like this."

I choked back my response. Getting defensive and

telling her to talk to her husband wouldn't help the situation and it would just hurt her more.

"Don't worry about it, okay." I pulled the door open and walked out.

The cold hit me as soon as I was outside. We'd had a mild winter and it wasn't more than ten below, but the folks liked their house warm. Too warm, I'd say, especially when a guy was going in and out, but it was their house and I had enough to argue about with the old man without getting into that. Still, the fresh air felt good, even if it was a bit of a shock to the system. I took a couple of deep breaths before heading across the yard to the barn.

The old man's barn was kind of like him, low and wide. Even the red it was painted sort of matched the colour of his face when he was pissed off. It was split up into pens for the cows instead of stalls, unplaned planks rubbed smooth by generations of cattle.

I heard the old man before I got to the barn door. He was talking low, almost crooning. I looked in the half-open door to where he was rubbing his hand up and down one of our cow's backs as she lay on a bed of fresh straw. Lucky was one of dad's more knot-headed cows, capable of getting into trouble when you would've thought it impossible. Which is how she got her name. This time Lucky had got tangled up in a fence somehow and tore some good-sized chunks out of her flank. Nothing serious if they didn't get infected. We'd managed to get her into the barn before supper and Dad had given her a shot of penicillin. Now to clean her up, leave her in the barn overnight and disinfect things one more time in the morning before letting her back into the pasture.

She stood quietly as Dad dabbed diluted Betadine on her wounds. The faint sharpness of the disinfectant mingled with the smells of manure and hay, bringing back memories of other cows, Caesareans, cleaning wounds in summer to keep the maggots out during fly season.

I decided to wait until he was finished. I leaned against the wall of the barn, shoved my hands into my parka pockets, and took deep breaths of cold air, trying to prepare myself. I looked out past the lights, across the field. Rows of bales blocked my view to the left, but to the right the field gleamed white in the moonlight. I could only see to the treeline. There was no watching your dog run away for three days up here, no distant horizons. Just fields that had been torn from the bush. Some good land, lots of rocks, and the bush never far away. My future.

Maybe.

Finally the old man came out of the barn, a disinfectant-stained cloth in one hand, the Betadine bottle in the other.

"Could've used some help in there," he said, his breath steaming in the cold.

"You had things under control. I would've just spooked her," I said, staying against the wall, trying to look casual. Calm and reasonable, that was the key.

"You intend to ignore all your chores like that now that you've got that new job?" he said. There it was, out in the open.

"Didn't know it was my chore. Lucky's one of your cows, remember?"

"Don't be a smartass. We work together. You know that." He shoved the disinfectant bottle into one pocket of his parka, the rag into the other, then pulled on his mitts.

I shook my head. "That's garbage and we both know it. How it works is that you give orders and I'm expected to obey them without comment. Anybody in the Armed Forces has more say in their lives than you're willing to give me."

"Bullshit. I co-signed for your land so you could learn some responsibility. You got all the say you want there."

I stared at him. He actually believed that. Talk about deluded.

"You helped me buy that land so I'd be tied to you," I said. "You didn't want me to get too far from the farm because then you couldn't control me anymore. You don't want a partner, you just want a farmhand you can count on not to quit."

"A farmhand I could fire when he started giving me the grief you give me."

"Grief? I'm trying to help the farm. How the hell is that grief?" I found myself coming off the wall, turning to face him head on. Shit. So much for calm and relaxed. Still, so far we were just circling around the same old arguments, the same worn grooves. Tonight though, I intended to skip out of those grooves.

"It's grief because you're not thinking. You jump on every fad that comes along." He was almost yelling now, trying to beat me down with volume. He'd begun to do that when I started refusing to take his shit and he'd never figured out that I could yell just as loud as he could. "You don't look at how much it'll cost or how we're going to pay for it." He pulled his right hand out of his mitt and started bringing fingers up as he went through the possibilities I'd brought up. "You want buffalo." One thick finger. "You want to go zero-till." A second finger. "You want to go to specialty crops." A third finger up, then he flipped his hand, waving away my ideas like you'd shoo away flies. "Breeding stock, chemicals, equipment, you think they grow on trees."

"And do you think we can just keep on going the way we're going. Give your head a shake." My voice had risen too, matching his volume. "We're not big enough to make a go of it, and buying enough land to be a serious threat would keep me in debt until I was old enough to retire. The only thing to do is to specialize. It's – " I stopped when I heard Lucky thrashing around inside the barn. I stepped back and looked in the door, the old man right behind me.

Lucky had gotten up and was backed into the corner of the pen, staring at us wildly.

"Smooth move," he said, fixing me with one of his glares, one of the ones I'd started getting when we began working together on the farm. Like the first time I rode the stooker behind the baler the year after Grandpa died. I was only fourteen, not the biggest of kids, but the old man made the bales big, eighty pounds and up, and set the tension so the twines were as tight as guitar strings. That made it hard enough to lift them, but then he wanted me to make fifteen bale stooks instead of ten like Grandpa did. I'd fought to get that last bale up, but how the hell do you lift something two-thirds of your weight, and awkward as hell, over your head? I'd gotten behind, had a couple of stooks collapse when I hit the unloading lever, and the old man hit the roof. "It's not that tough. Grandpa was pampering you." I shrunk in on myself, withering as he glared down at me, his words lashing me. Now I realized he was glaring *up* at me and I felt something open up inside. I smiled.

"Look after your cow," I said calmly, meeting his glare with a newfound confidence. I had his measure now. Time to show him that.

"Don't think we're finished," he growled as he pushed past me into the barn.

As if I'd be so lucky. I leaned against the doorjamb and watched him as he braced himself against the pen's gate and talked to the spooked cow.

"Easy, girl, nothing to worry about. Relax. Nothing to concern you..." He kept talking to her until she calmed down. He was good at that, good with animals. He'd even been good with me as a kid. It was only me as an adult, an equal, that he had problems with. Anything to do with the farm and he turned into the world's biggest prick.

"Outside," he growled at me when he was done.

I nodded, then walked out the door. I strolled down to the corner of the corral, putting a few yards between us and the barn. I turned to face him. Time to finish this.

"So, you're going to go it on your own?" He kept his voice low, but it grated. Must have killed him to keep the volume down. It'd been one of his favourite tricks lately. "I've never heard anything so fucking stupid in my life."

"Stupid? Not really." I looked out over the corral at the fields again. "I've been thinking a lot about things since last year. I didn't know what to do with you, with the farm. I didn't want to be a hired hand for you anymore, didn't want to be told what to do, to be ignored every time I spoke. So, I had to find a way to make my farm work for me."

"Your job?" he said, interrupting me. "Do you really think that some part-time woodworking job is going to keep your farm going? Christ, don't be stupid."

No, this time I wasn't going to take the bait. I continued as calmly and evenly as I had before he jumped in.

"Mr. Lambert, John, he wants me to go full-time. With a raise. Says I do good work." I looked at him again. The glare was gone now, but I wasn't sure what had replaced it. It wasn't worry. Too bad. I could've used worry. "Anyway, I've been thinking about it seriously, crunching the numbers, trying to decide what I should do."

"You should tell him to fuck off," the old man said harshly. "You've got enough work to do here. You don't have time for more in town."

"Not if I keep on doing all I've been doing here," I agreed. "But why would I want to? I could have a boss who listens, who respects my opinion, who gives me responsibility. All that while I'm doing something I love doing. Tell me how you compete with that?"

"Because I'm the one leaving you the farm," he snapped. "Is Lambert leaving you the business?" He stopped, his eyes gleaming triumphantly.

"No," I agreed, "he isn't. But there's the possibility if I decide to sell the Penman quarter that I could buy him out some day." That was pure bullshit, but I wanted to hit the old man hard while I had him off balance.

"You wouldn't. You love the farm too much."

"The farm sure. But there's a big difference between loving the farm and loving farming. I figure I could rent out the Penman quarter and use my other two quarters for the cattle. I've got the fields on them to grow feed and hay and still could take off a bit of crop for cash. Wouldn't make a fortune, but I can live on the job money. I just don't want to be losing money from farming. I've done too much of that."

"Are you nuts?" He stepped toward me, crowding me against the fence, getting right in my face. "Do you want to lose everything your grandfather and I worked for? Do you want to give all that away on a whim?" He was yelling now, his face reddening.

"Fuck, there's your answer right there," I yelled, stepping away from the fence, snow crunching underfoot. I crowded him back and we stood toe to toe, no give in either one of us, the volume cranked, the cow forgotten. "You didn't mention all the work *I've* done and you automatically assumed that because I thought of it, it's some sort of fly-by-night idea. Newsflash, Dad, I've been thinking about nothing but this for months. I figured out what I wanted. I want control of my life. You're always yapping at me to be a man, well, here I go. I'm taking responsibility for my life. Isn't that what a man does?"

"You're not being a man. You're being selfish. All you're thinking about is yourself." His face was red right up to the edge of his cap now.

"How is that any different from you? Your farm, your rules. You can say you're doing it all for me, but that's bullshit. It's all about you."

"You ungrateful, little..." He forced his voice down as Lucky mooed.

"Bastard? That was the word you were going to use, wasn't it?" My tone was almost conversational now. "Don't worry, I've been called worse by better men." I saw his hands curl into fists. This was new. For once I was definitely threatening him. Time to go in for the kill.

"So, here's the deal," I said quickly, cutting him off before he could start in on me again. "We can go one of two ways on this. You can agree to work with me, give me help trying out some new things and get rid of your idea of buying a bunch of new land together or I can go to work for Mr. Lambert full-time, and rent out the quarter and hunker down to take care of my own and you can go it alone." I bit back the urge to say, "You can go fuck yourself." I had to give him at least a half-fair chance to make a decision.

"You're giving me an ultimatum?" he said incredulously, too surprised to even yell. "In my yard, you dare tell me how things are going to be? You're fucking nuts."

"Maybe," I said, " but since when are two choices an ultimatum?"

"If you think I'm going to let you tell me how to run my farm – "

"Your farm! That's the problem. It's not Mom's, it's not mine, it's yours. Never ours. I can't live like that anymore."

"And you think you can retreat to some little dream world and make a go of it?" He shook his head. "That's even stupider than any of your other plans."

"Maybe so, but it's what I'm going to do."

"You're bluffing." He sounded sure, confident that I could never get out from under his control.

"I've talked to Greg Hicks already. He's willing to take the Penman quarter for a year and then we can talk about it again." Hicks had surprised me. I thought he'd want to lock in having the land for two or three years before he took it on, but he'd been good about it. That was one of the reasons I could take a stab at the job and stick to cattle.

"He wouldn't. I'll talk to his dad. John won't let Greg do it if I ask him not to." Now I could hear the desperation in his voice. He was on the ropes. Question was, would he go down or not?

"It's business, Dad. Greg's father understands that. And Greg is his own man. He was a real partner to John years ago." I locked eyes with Dad, seeing neither ice nor anger there for the first time all night. "So, what do you say? Are you going to work with me or not?"

He lowered his eyes. Yes! I had him. I finally had him. Then he shook his head.

"No," he said, "I don't think so. This will all fall apart on you before you know it. I'll just wait until you come crawling back."

I stared at him in disbelief and felt myself go cold inside. What would it take to get through to him? Then I realized it was a lost cause. I'd spent the last ten years we'd farmed together trying to get his approval. It had been this Holy Grail for me and I had about as much chance of finding it as the *Monty Python* guys did. Maybe I couldn't get it because he didn't have it to give. Maybe he just couldn't say it, or maybe he couldn't admit that I could succeed without him. But it wasn't going to happen. I'd have to rub his nose in it, show him through others that I had succeeded. Then maybe I'd hear him tell me that I'd done a good job.

"Don't hold your breath," I said. I turned and started to walk away.

"You'll be back," he yelled at me. I kept on walking toward the house. I heard Lucky's moo in the still winter air, then the slam of the barn door. I wondered who was going to calm down who.

Mom stood on the back step, shivering. I didn't know if it was from the cold or from the fight.

"Go inside," I said. "Everything will be all right."

"Are you sure?" She looked toward the barn, her face ashen. "He's such a proud man..."

I shrugged. His pride wasn't my problem. He could pull the stick out of his own ass. I had to worry about myself. Now that the fight was over, all that was left was the living.

I called Hicks as soon as I got home.

MAKING
THE CALL

Ski heard Terri's car turn into the yard. His stomach was full of butterflies and he realized he hadn't felt like this on a date since he was fourteen. The stakes on this date were a lot higher though. It was likely the only chance he'd get to convince Terri he'd changed, that she could trust him not to hurt her.

Stephie was out of the car almost before it stopped.

"Ski!" She ran to him and he scooped her up in his arms.

"Jeez, what've you been eating the last couple of weeks, rocks?"

Stephie stuck her tongue out at him. "You're just getting weaker," she said.

"Yeah, that must be it." Ski looked at Terri as she got out of the car. He felt a twinge. She looked so beautiful, but her face was cold, set. He'd given her reason to feel that way, but why wouldn't she give him a chance to redeem himself?

"Hey, Terri, how are you?"

"Fine." She looked around. "What do you want me to do? We've only got an hour before everyone else gets here."

"Lots of time," Ski said. "Greg helped me haul some firewood, a couple of benches and a picnic table down to the old Barton yard yesterday. All we need to do is get the food ready, harness the horses and away we go."

Terri looked at Ski suspiciously. He tried to look innocent. Even if she figured out that he'd got them out here early to work on her it wasn't like she could just get in the car and leave. It was Stephie's birthday today, and the sleigh ride and wiener roast was part of Ski's gift to her. Terri hadn't liked it when Ski spoke directly to Stephie about the sleigh ride and for a while he thought she'd say no, but Stephie had stayed on her and Stephie's cousin Ryan had jumped in when Stephie tired, and together they wore Terri down. She'd finally relented, but only on one condition, that Ski didn't talk about the two of them. He'd agreed and for the last week had been thinking of indirect ways to show her he'd changed.

Ryan had gotten out of the back of the car while Ski was looking at Terri. There was a huge grin plastered on his face, matching the one on Stephie's. Looked like they missed Ski and the farm as much as he missed the two of them.

"How's it going?" Ski said, shifting Stephie to the crook of his left arm and holding his hand out to shake Ryan's.

"Great," the twelve-year-old said. "When can I take the Ski-Doo out?"

"Ryan!" Terri fixed her nephew with narrow eyes. "That's rude. And Stephie, you're not a baby anymore. Ski can't be carrying you."

"She's not that heavy," Ski said. He realized his mistake as soon as the words were out of his mouth.

"Are you telling me how to raise my daughter?" she snapped.

Christ, she'd come primed for a fight. "Of course not." Ski set Stephie down. "I just don't mind."

"Well I do." Terri glared at Ski.

"Mom, you promised," Stephie whined. "You said you wouldn't argue with Ski."

Terri took a deep breath. "Sorry, you're right." She smiled. It looked very forced to Ski, but Stephie didn't notice.

"Ski, I want you to promise too," Stephie said. She wore the same stubborn expression that Ski had seen on her mother's face so many times.

"I wouldn't do anything to mess up your birthday," Ski said, trying to think of a way to talk to Terri without it turning into a fight.

"That's not a promise."

"No, it isn't." Ski crossed his finger over his chest. "Cross my heart and hope to die, I won't fight with your mom today."

"Good." Stephie nodded her head firmly, then looked at her mom. "You didn't cross your heart, Mom."

Terri smiled wanly. "Cross my heart and hope to die, I won't argue with Ski," she said, mirroring Ski's gesture with her mittened hand.

"Good," Stephie said again. Sure that peace would

reign, she immediately forgot about it. "Where's Deputy?" she said, referring to Ski's dog.

"Sleeping down by the barn last time I saw him. He's getting even lazier than Ryan."

"Hey, watch it." Ryan had the trunk of Terri's car open and was taking out bags of groceries. "Did you forget who got the best shots in last time we traded zingers?"

"You had help from Mac and your aunt, if I recall."

"Doesn't matter, I still showed you who was smarter." Ryan carried the bags up the steps. "Where do you want these?"

"The coolers are in there, you can put the food in them."

"Let me do that," Terri said. "All you and Stephie could talk about on the way out here was the horses, so go see them. I'll take care of the picnic stuff." She looked at Ski. "You can make sure they're okay around the horses." She got a worried look on her face. "Max isn't around is he?"

"No, I took him over to my cousin Nolan's yesterday," Ski said. "You know I wouldn't have him in the yard with a bunch of kids around."

Terri nodded and took the bags from Ryan.

"Why not?" Ryan said. "I like Mad Max."

"Me too," Ski said, "but he's not the steadiest of horses. Too headstrong and wild. Someone might get kicked or bitten. I'd rather not take the chance."

"Can we go over and see him after?" Ryan asked. Terri had already opened the door of the house and taken the groceries in. Ski looked after her with regret for a second, then led the kids down the trail through the spruce to the barnyard. Coffee, his second riding horse, was in the pasture by the barn, while Beau and Belle, his team of matched Clydesdales was in the barn. He'd stripped the work harness from them this morning after chores and had spent over an hour getting them spruced up for the sleigh ride. He even had a couple of surprises for Stephie.

"Deputy." Stephie ran forward to where the old dog was lifting himself out of a pile of straw by the barn door. She wrapped her arms around the old collie's neck and gave him a hug. The dog's tail started wagging frantically as he pushed himself further into her embrace.

"Looks like he missed you too," Ski said, reaching down to give Deputy a pat.

"Yeah, he probably just misses being spoiled rotten," Ryan said.

Ski reached out and tousled the boy's hair. "Be nice, Ryan. It's her birthday today."

"Hey, watch the hair," Ryan said, pulling back from Ski.

Ski laughed. "Christ, you're getting worse than a woman with your hair."

"That's just because it looks so damn good."

"Watch the language," Ski said, mildly. "Stephie doesn't need to pick up any of your bad habits."

"Not like I picked it up from you."

"Bull. I don't swear around you two."

"Not like the Dick does," Ryan said. "You slip once in a while, though."

"Maybe once in a while," Ski said. "Don't let Terri

hear you calling your dad the Dick. She'll tear a strip off me big time then."

"Why not? That's what she calls him."

"Only when she figures you can't hear. She figures you should have some respect for your dad."

"Why?" Ryan asked.

Ski shrugged. Damned if he could figure that out. The Dick's real name was Richard, but since the first time Ski heard Terri call him the Dick he hadn't been able to think of him as anything else. The Dick's job came first with him. He was proud of working sixty or seventy hour weeks, then having no energy to do anything but lie on the couch and watch sports. Ryan was barely on his dad's radar since he didn't have any interest in sports. Kid liked books and animals. He was like a junkie with books and Terri was his dealer. Ski took care of the animals. And the snowmobiling. And listening to Ryan. As far as Ski was concerned Ryan could come to the farm any time, even if Terri didn't come back to him. He liked the kid, and Ryan needed someone to play uncle.

"Who do you have in the barn?" Stephie asked. She was walking to the barn door, Deputy wriggling at her side.

"The Bluebells," Ski said. The horses were really called Beau and Belle but Ski's niece had got Beau mixed up as Blue and then the team became the Bluebells. Stephie had picked it up from Candace and Ski figured the team would be the Bluebells until the day they died.

"The Bluebells? Goody." She looked at Ski and put on her sweetest look. "Can I curry them?"

"In a bit," Ski said. "I've got to put some wood in the fire first. Then we can curry them before I harness them."

"You mean we harness them," Ryan said.

"No, I mean me." Ski smiled at Ryan to take the sting out of the words. "I've got some new harness and it's even heavier than the old stuff you tried with last year." Not to mention Ryan was only a couple of inches taller than last year and the shoulders of the horses were over a foot above his head. Hell, some days Ski had a hard enough time getting the harness over the horses' backs.

"I can do up the buckles, can't I?" Ryan said. "And hook the chains to the sleigh."

"If you promise to be careful."

"Of course I will. But Beau and Belle aren't dangerous."

"Not on purpose, but they make twenty of you. If they step on your foot, you'll be in a world of hurt."

"You think I don't know that? Jeez Ski, I'm twelve, not six."

"Sorry, I forgot how ancient you were."

"Nah, you're ancient," Ryan said, drawing himself up to his full height and puffing out his chest. "I'm just mature."

Ski hid a grin as he faked another try at Ryan's hair.

"Well, Mr. Mature, grab an armful of wood, while I knock down the coals."

"Yes, sir, Mr. Ancient Guy sir."

Ski rolled his eyes. "Just get the wood, smart aleck."

"Just about slipped. Thought you didn't swear around us."

"Guess I'm out of practice. Now get the wood."

"Yes, boss." Ryan strolled over to the wood pile, whistling merrily. Stephie was playing with Deputy, the dog wriggling and jumping all around her, spazzing as only a collie could spaz. It felt so right that Ski had to stop and watch the kids for a second. They belonged here. Terri belonged here.

Ski squatted by the water trough and opened the door to the firebox. He jabbed at the coals inside with a piece of wood, jamming them down. He took the wood Ryan handed him and shoved it in until the box was full. He waited to see if it would catch, then put his arm out to stop Ryan from kneeling down and blowing on the fire.

"You're wearing good clothes," Ski said. "Your aunt Terri would have a fit if you got horse shit on them ten minutes after you got here."

"You mean crap, don't you?"

Shit. Crap. Damn, he knew how to talk around kids. He just had to concentrate on it.

"Whatever." Ski kneeled and blew on the coals. In short order, flames were flickering among the logs.

"Where's the gas can?" Ryan said, looking around the trough area. "You can't tell me you actually learned how to make a fire without gas. Not in the couple of months since the last time I saw you."

"Very funny," Ski said, swinging the firebox's door shut and latching it. "I know how to build a fire without gas."

"Yeah, Ryan, Ski doesn't use gas to start fires," Stephie said, standing beside Ski. He started to smile. "He uses diesel fuel."

Ryan burst out laughing as he looked at Ski's face.

"Thanks a lot, Stephie," Ski said.

"You're welcome." Stephie smiled at Ski. "Can we see the Bluebells now?" She looked at the far end of the pasture. "Or Coffee and Double-Double?"

"How about the big team first, then we'll wander down to see Coffee and the foal."

"How come she hasn't come up to see us?"

"She's had her oats already and a big drink of water. She'll probably come up here later to see if she can get a treat or find a little girl to spoil her." The quarter horse mare was Ski's second riding horse. Not as fast or fun as Mad Max, but a lot more stable and trustworthy. You didn't have to be on your toes the whole time you rode her. And she could go all day. Max would run himself out early, then he'd be useless until he'd rested for awhile. The last couple of years Ski had found himself riding Coffee more and more and Max less and less.

Even his cousin had noticed. "You're getting old, Ski. Can't handle a real horse," Nolan had said. "Time to sell him to me."

"I've got sugar," Stephie said, patting her parka pocket.

"The horses will like that." Ski stepped through the large barn door. He'd left it open because he'd used Beau and Belle in the morning and didn't want the barn to get too warm or the team overheated.

The barn was dim inside, the only light the sunlight streaming in through the open doors and through the one small, dust-covered window. Ski flicked the light switch and two bare bulbs lit. Beau and Belle stood in separate stalls, their coats gleaming in the dim light, ribbons braided into their manes and tails. Stephie squealed when she saw the ribbons.

"Ribbons! I love ribbons." She gave Ski's legs a quick hug, then started to run toward Belle's stall.

"Whoa, there," Ski said, catching Stephie by the arm. "You know better than to run behind a horse."

"But Belle would never kick me."

"You don't know what she might do if she's surprised. You've got to give her some warning." He led Stephie into the empty stall next to Belle's, the one he used for his harness. He watched her face and was rewarded by her eyes widening as she saw the harness there now.

"Ski, it's beautiful. Where'd you get it."

"Mac lent it to me. It was his grandpa's. I've had my eye on it for a while, but I've never been able to convince Mac to sell it to me." The harness gleamed midnight black, the leather polished to a high sheen. It was a far cry from the plain brown working harness that Ski had always used.

Stephie ran her hands over the leather, then found the other treat Ski had got from Mac. A high clear note echoed through the barn as she flicked one of the silver bells on the harness.

"Do you like them?" Ski asked.

"I love them."

"Well, Mac told me to tell you Happy Birthday. Said he hoped you liked them."

"Is Mac coming today?"

"No, he's down in Saskatoon visiting his brother, but we can phone him after."

"Good. I like Mac." She turned to stroke the harness some more, leaning her head close to look at the silver in it.

Ski's eyebrows had risen when Stephie made her comment about Mac. Weren't a lot of kids Mac didn't scare. At least not girls. Ski's nieces thought he looked mean. Of course when Stephie saw Mac he was in the kitchen at Ski's telling stories and swapping smart-ass comments with Ryan.

"I thought you didn't like ribbons on horses," Ryan said quietly from Ski's side. "Too girly."

"Doesn't matter what I think," Ski said. "This is Stephie's day."

"Do I get a sleigh ride when it's my birthday?" Ryan said.

"Sure," Ski said, before he remembered Ryan's birthday was in August.

Ryan laughed. "I'm going to make you keep that promise," he said.

"Go ahead. It's going to be the horses who have the hardest time of it."

"You wouldn't do that to Beau and Belle, would you," Stephie said, frowning at Ski.

"Of course not. Ryan and I are just goofing around."

"Okay. Can I curry Belle?" She picked the curry-comb out of the manger and started pulling hair out of its teeth.

"I've already done them, but you can give them a few minutes before I harness them." Ski picked Stephie up under the arms and lifted her so she could stand on one of the planks that made up the walls of the stalls. He kept his arm around her even as she leaned forward and ran the currycomb over Belle's back. The big mare turned her head and let out a low whinny.

"She likes it," Stephie said. "Can I do her tail, Ski? Please?"

"I don't know if that's a good idea, Stephie."

"She likes it, you know she does."

"I don't know that she likes it that much. Besides, I did it already." He'd figured she'd ask so he'd been extra careful to get all the knots out of Belle's tail. He didn't know where Stephie had got the bright idea that horses liked having their tails combed, but she was stubborn and he'd given up trying to change her mind.

"Please, Ski," Stephie said. She gave him an ingratiating smile. "It's my birthday, remember?"

Ouch. He'd walked into that one. He looked at Belle. She was always steady and she'd been worked today so any piss and vinegar in her would've been worked out. Also, the ribbons meant there wasn't a lot that Stephie could do. It would be safe and a few quick strokes should make her happy.

"Okay, but just for a minute. I've got to get the harness on and you don't want me to bonk you in the head when I'm swinging it on."

"You wouldn't do that," Stephie said, wiggling out of Ski's grasp to clamber down the stall's planks like they were a ladder. Ski had to grab her arm before she stepped into Belle's stall.

"What did I tell you about going into a horse's stall?" he said.

"Never go into a stall if you're not here."

"And?"

"Always let you go in first," she said, then burst out, "but you let Ryan into the stalls by himself."

"Ryan's bigger than you are and he doesn't get excited and careless. You get a bit older, a bit bigger and we'll see about changing the rules, but until then you stay out of the stalls without me around."

"It's because Ryan's a boy, isn't it?" Stephie said sullenly.

"No." Ski took a deep breath. "I said I wouldn't argue with your mom today and I won't argue with you either." He smiled at Stephie. "Besides, Belle's waiting to have her tail done."

"Is that a good idea?" Terri said from behind them. Ski turned his head to see her outlined in the doorway.

"Why not? She's done it before."

"It just makes me nervous. They're so big. They could hurt her without meaning to, or even trying."

"Ski's already given me that line, Aunt Terri," Ryan said. "He's making us be careful."

"Yeah, mom, you know Ski wouldn't let Belle hurt me," Stephie said.

"You're assuming he has control over everything and can stop people from getting hurt," Terri said.

Ski wished she'd step into the barn so he could see her face because all of a sudden he didn't think she was talking about the horses and the kids anymore.

"Of course I can't control everything," Ski said. He stepped into Belle's stall, patted her on the rump to let her know he was there. Belle looked over her shoulder briefly and went back to munching on the hay in the manger. He had to give her a shove to get her to step sideways, so she was against the far side of the stall. "Okay, Stephie, it's safe now," he said, standing by Belle's back leg so if she tried to kick he'd take it instead of Stephie. Stephie stood close to Ski and ran the comb through the hair on Belle's tail. Ski watched for a second then looked at Terri.

"Like I said, I can't control everything and people are going to get hurt, but I've learned to take precautions. I worked the team this morning so they wouldn't have any piss and vinegar in them, I curried Belle myself a while ago so there wouldn't be any knots that might make her kick because I knew Stephie would probably want to do Belle's tail. I lent Max to Nolan so he wouldn't bite the kids when they tried to pet him or kick them if they climbed into the pasture." He kept his gaze fixed on Terri's silhouette, trying to gauge her reaction to his words. "Sure I was a bit careless when they first came out here, but I had to learn they weren't farm kids, that I couldn't treat them like kids who lived out here. Once I got that into my thick skull I figured out what I had to do so they wouldn't get hurt. Wasn't only me, though. They had to learn too, and meet me partway." There, he'd made a couple of points and Stephie hadn't even noticed. Ryan, on the other hand, had faded into the tack stall and was watching Terri intently.

"It seems they've had to meet you more than halfway," Terri said. "And they still got hurt a couple of times."

"Ski didn't hurt us," Ryan said. Ski didn't figure he

understood completely what was going on, but he was willing to take the help.

"What are you guys talking about?" Stephie said.

"Nothing important," Ski said. "Another couple of strokes and then I'll have to start harnessing them."

"Can Ryan and I go down and see Coffee and Double-Double then?"

"Sure," Ski said. That'd give him the perfect opportunity to talk to Terri.

"Yeah, let's go see Coffee," Ryan said. He glared at his aunt. "We might not get the chance again."

"Ryan – " There was pain and anger in Terri's voice.

"Ryan, don't," Ski said. "That not arguing on Stephie's birthday applies to you too." He smiled at the boy. "Besides, you're always welcome out here. Just give me a call and we can set up a visit."

"What about me?" The whine was back in Stephie's voice.

"You'd have to ask your mom, pun'kin, but I'll always be happy to see you."

"Ski – " Terri's voice was hard-edged.

"You said you wouldn't argue," Stephie said, glaring at her mom.

"I'm not – "

"Sounds like it to me. Ski's not arguing so why do you have to?"

Terri plastered another forced smile on her face. Her face would crack if she had to do that too often, Ski figured.

"We were just having a discussion," Terri said. "Why don't you go see Coffee and I'll help Ski."

"You're just trying to get rid of us so you can fight," Stephie said.

"Honest, I'm not."

"You won't yell at him anymore, will you? I don't like it and you could scare the Bluebells."

Terri smiled again, a little more real this time. "I wouldn't want to scare the Bluebells," she said. "I won't yell at Ski. Can I talk to him, though?"

"Yes, but I can hear you if you yell."

"I know you can, hon." Terri gave Stephie a quick hug. "Now go see Coffee and her colt."

"Okay, but no arguing." Stephie gave Terri a dirty look, then shook her head. "And Double-Double is a filly, not a colt," she said before stomping out the door, Ryan trailing after her, looking over his shoulder at Ski and Terri, a worried expression on his face.

Terri waited until the kids had climbed through the rails on the pasture fence by the trough.

"Don't you ever use my daughter against me," she said in a low voice.

"I wasn't." Ski kept his voice low too. "I meant it when I said that Stephie could come out here. Double-Double is still hers and I still am going to train him."

"You think that's going to convince me you've changed? You must figure I didn't learn anything in the time I went out with you."

"And you must figure I didn't learn anything either. Christ, Terri, what is it going to take to get you to give me another chance? Or are you even willing to give me another chance?"

Terri had stepped into the barn out of Stephie and

Ryan's sight. Her face came out of the shadows so Ski could see the play of emotions across it. He could also see the one emotion that he'd never seen, the one he'd finally learned how to see only weeks before.

Fear.

Not fear of Ski, but of what he could do to her. It was fear of being hurt. It was a fear that had grown out of her marriage and that he himself had fed with all his stupid behaviour, his refusal to grow up, his ongoing wish to be the cowboy, the freewheeling, independent stud who didn't need anybody, who was rough and tough and could ride anything with two legs or four, and the wilder the ride the better.

"Terri, the last thing I want to do is hurt you," he said softly.

"I want to believe you, I really do, but..."

"But I've given you lots of reasons not to." He sighed. "I know. I've had a lot of time to think about things the last few weeks and I know you've got no reason to believe me when I say I've changed, but I have."

"They're all just words, Ski." Pain etched Terri's face. "How can I believe them, when they're the same words I've heard half a dozen times before? 'Terri, I don't look at other women anymore,' 'Terri, I want to settle down,' 'Terri, I'd never do anything to hurt you.' I can't let you have the chance to do that to me any more. I can't, I won't, spend any more nights crying my eyes out over you."

Ski leaned back against the side of Belle's stall and closed his eyes. Shit. He'd always thought of Terri as so tough, so strong. He'd never seen how much of it was a front, a shield against pain. Like Ryan or Mac used the quick lip and the storytelling. Or the way Brad MacAllister stuck his nose in a book for the same reason.

"I can't guarantee I won't hurt you," he finally said. "I can't promise that, any more than I can promise that the kids will never get hurt around the farm. Bumps and scrapes come with the territory. What I can promise you is that I'll do my damnedest not to hurt you, just like I've done my damnedest to make sure the farm is safe for the kids."

"Damn it, weren't you listening? Those are just more words."

"Fine, then I'll show you something." Ski grabbed Terri by the hand, pulled her behind him to the water trough. He'd thought of this before, when he knew Terri was coming. He let go of her hand, knelt and opened the door to the firebox. The heat washed over him as the flames licked around the doorway. Ski pulled a paper bag out of his pocket.

"I know you heard Mac yap about my stash, didn't you?" he said.

She nodded, face blank, unreadable.

"Well, here it is. Every phone number I've collected over the years, every matchbook cover, every napkin, every coaster. I should've thrown them out last year when we got serious, but you were right, I was never willing to take any big steps. Well, now I am." He thrust his hand into the bag, yanked out a handful of paper, tossed it into the flames.

No reaction from Terri.

Another handful.

No reaction.

Finally he threw in the bag.

Still no reaction.

He watched as his stash turned to ash.

Not a twitch from Terri.

Ski closed the firedoor, stood. "I love you Terri. I don't need other women. I don't want other women."

Finally, her facade cracked. "I'm sorry Ski, it's not enough. How do I know you didn't save some of the numbers? How do I know you didn't write them down somewhere?"

"Christ, Terri, what do I have to do, run through fire? You've got to trust me a bit, sooner or later, or we don't stand a chance."

"I know," Terri said quietly. She stared bleakly down the pasture. "If only it was as simple for us as it is for them." She nodded her head toward where Stephie and Ryan were playing with Coffee and Double-Double.

Ski looked over to where the kids were petting the foal. Coffee stood nearby watching the three youngsters indulgently. Double-Double was taking a lump of sugar out of Stephie's hand. Her giggle carried up the pasture. Finally Stephie looked up and saw the adults watching her.

"Can I ride Coffee?" she yelled, causing Double-Double to jump back. She turned and spoke to the filly softly, holding her hand out, calming her down. Ski nodded. She'd learned well.

"Your call," Ski said to Terri.

"Is she okay with the colt around?" Terri said.

"Filly," Ski said. "A young female horse is a filly."

"Whatever," Terri said. "Is it safe?"

"Yeah. It's only when you try to take her out of the pasture and leave Double-Double behind that she starts fighting you. Ryan leading her up the pasture won't be a problem." Ski smiled sadly. "Besides, I took her for a ride yesterday. Wanted to take any edge she might have off her."

Terri looked at Ski through narrowed eyes. "You really worked to make this day special, didn't you?"

"More than you could possibly know," he said. He watched her carefully, trying to read her face, stopping himself from reading anything into what he saw. The moment stretched out, agonizingly long, until Terri broke away, turning her head to look at the kids.

"Be careful, Stephie," she called.

Ski turned to watch the kids. Ryan had led Coffee to the fence and Stephie scrambled up the rails, then grabbed a handful of the mare's mane as she jumped up and swung her leg over Coffee's back. Once she was settled in she nodded to Ryan and he started to lead the horse toward the end of the corral where Ski and Terri stood.

"See, I can ride," Stephie called to the adults.

Ryan snorted. "It's not like she's Mad Max. Now he's a real horse."

"No he's not. He's a jughead."

Terri looked at Ski and raised an eyebrow. "A jughead?"

"I couldn't call him a stupid pig-headed bastard in front of Stephie, could I?"

That almost got a smile from Terri. "Feeling complimentary towards him aren't you?" she said.

He grinned. "Yeah, I guess so." He watched Ryan lead Coffee around the corral, Stephie clinging to the mare's back. "You know, I used to love Max, but people change. I'm too old to be fighting with a horse all the time. I want one that works with me, not against me." He paused for a second. Actions, not words.

"Look, Nolan has been bugging me for months to sell Max to him. All I have to do is make one phone call. Just say the word."

She looked at him silently. Before she could reply, they heard a car pull into the yard.

"I guess you better get the horses harnessed," she said. "We've got company."

TIME OUT

MacAllister saw his fist fly past the little girl's head and bury itself into the drywall. He felt the rush as he had then, the blaze of anger that he rode like a bucking bronco, always only one careless moment away from being tossed into the haze of rage, the swinging of fists, the only cure the crunch of something, someone, under his knuckles. He took a deep breath, willed his fists to unclench. That had been a long time ago. He'd been hungover. The kid had been a monster. Everything was different now. He was different.

He had to be.

"You okay, Uncle Andy?" Mac's nephew, Tyler, looked up at him, worry on his small face.

"Yah, Tye, just a little out of it." Mac leaned back in the chair and took a deep breath. Today wasn't like that day with Nicole. Back then, he'd drunk way too much the night before and wasn't ready for his soon-to-be-ex-girlfriend's bratty kid getting in his face. He'd taken a punch at her and only pulled it at the last minute, driving his fist through the drywall by her head instead of into the five-year-old's face. Things were different today. The house was bigger, the kid better behaved, and, most importantly, the kid was a MacAllister. No way he could hit one of his own.

But had that ever stopped Gramps or the old man? Well, maybe the old man sometimes, but never Gramps. Damn Brad for sticking him with his kid like this. Bad enough that Brad had been riding his ass the last few days about dealing with Gramps. He'd buried the old bastard. He didn't need to dig him up again so he could deal with his feelings. Especially when the only feeling it seemed to bring up was the anger that had driven him into fight after fight in the first place. All it had taken was the slightest thing to set him off. That was the last thing he needed. That and getting stuck in a replay of the day with Nicole. What was Brad thinking? He knew what had happened with Nicole.

No, it wasn't fair. But there wasn't much else he could do. The phone call had been so sudden, the car accident unanticipated. Brad had to get Kathleen to University Hospital where her sister was and there hadn't been time to get a sitter. And in this blizzard not much was moving anyway. Mac had even talked Brad into taking his truck. It might be old, but the tires were good and it had four-wheel drive and weight on the back end. A lot better for the drifted-in streets than Brad's little Camry.

"Uncle Andy, I'm hungry."

Mac looked at his watch. Quarter to five. Getting on to suppertime and the kid hadn't eaten since lunch.

"Yah, okay. A peanut butter and jam sandwich good enough?"

"Mom doesn't like me to have peanut butter and jam too much. Says I'm supposed to eat my vegetables."

"Which would you sooner have?"

"The peanut butter and jam."

"Then," Mac winked at Tye, "we just won't tell her, will we?"

"Okay."

Mac grunted. This was the way kids were supposed to be, well-behaved and obedient. Not like Nicole. He remembered her standing there, staring straight at him, defiant. Tye was probably more the way Gramps figured him and Brad were supposed to be when he whaled on them with his chunk of harness leather. And Brad and Kathleen did it without laying a hand on the kid. Carrying things a bit too far, but he was their kid. Mac figured he could go along with their ideas for as long as he was with them. And for today him and the kid could just do whatever each other wanted. No friction that way. Of course, he'd tried doing that with Nicole, watching cartoons and playing Nintendo with her. Look how well that had worked out.

No. It'd work now. No friction, no anger. No anger, no fists.

Mac strode into the kitchen, Tye following him slowly. Mac looked back.

"You want your sandwich, don't you?"

"Yeah." The kid came in and climbed up into the breakfast nook. Mac frowned. Thought he'd finally got through to the kid. Was talking to him normally without his parents around and Tye didn't have that look of worry that he used to have.

Worry. Mac shook his head. Who was he kidding? The kid had been afraid of him. And he hadn't been any help, flying off the handle when he was arguing with Brad, especially the way they'd been going at it the last couple of days. Kid had probably been hiding up in his room not knowing what was going on, what to do. Mac remembered that from when the old man had come home after a couple of weeks on the road, half-pissed and expecting the old lady to wait on him hand and foot. They'd gone at it hammer and tongs and Brad had been the one who cried. Mac remembered slipping out of his bed, creeping over to Brad's bed and shushing him. Brad would grab his hand and Mac would sit there, holding his hand and shivering in the dark, until Brad fell asleep, then he'd slip back into his own bed.

"Uncle Mac?"

"Yeah?" Mac looked at Tye and frowned. The kid was curled up in the nook, arms around his knees, so much like Nicole curled up on her bed that day that Mac's breath caught in his throat. He closed his eyes for a second, then looked at Tye again.

Now the kid looked like Brad, all those years ago. Their mother's looks mostly, the MacAllister in him limited. Thank God for small mercies, Mac thought. Instead of being tall and rangy, Brad and Tye were smaller, fine-boned, with Mac's mom's thick chestnut hair and pale blue eyes. It was the eyes that sent a chill through Mac. Brad's eyes, with the same fear that Brad had when Gramps was around. God, he couldn't be as bad as Gramps, could he?

"Why don't you like me?" Tye asked in a small voice.

Mac stopped, stunned, knife in one hand, peanut butter jar in the other.

"What?"

"Why don't you like me?" Tye's voice was almost a whisper now.

"I like you. Of course I like you. Why do you think I don't?"

"The way you look at me. You're always mad at me."

"Mad – no, Tye, you're all wrong about that." Or was he? Kid was part of the world and, like Brad told him, Mac had been mad at the world for a long time. "I'm not mad at you. It's just me. I'm – not happy. It's not you, it's not anybody."

"Not Dad? You fight with him all the time."

"That's different. That's adult stuff. And I'm not mad at your dad. I know he means well." Except he insisted on playing shrink when Mac would just as soon leave all that shit in the past. Especially that day with Nicole. Wasn't anything to be gained by picking at all those old scabs, so why bother? None of this was about Gramps. Old Red was dead and buried. This was about Mac.

"But you're always frowning all the time and your face is all tight." Tye had pushed himself even farther into the nook until he was right against the wall. Hiding. Jesus, had he been that bad?

"I've got a lot on my mind, okay." Shit, he felt the burning building up in his belly, the way it had when

Nicole refused to turn down her ghetto blaster. His heart beat faster and he felt his muscles tighten.

No, not here, not with Tye. Nicole had been a mistake, one he wouldn't make again.

He slathered peanut butter on the bread, scooped jam out of the jar and spread it on, slapped the second piece of bread on top. What else? Kathleen would use a plate. Mac dropped the sandwich on a small plate and took it to Tye.

"There you go. You want some milk with that?" Mac tried to relax. He smiled at Tye, but it felt fake even to him, like someone had hooked him back of the ears with fishhooks and was giving his face a good tug.

"Yes, please," Tye said quietly.

Mac poured two glasses of milk, took them back to the nook, sat down across from Tye. He noticed Tye was only nibbling at his sandwich.

"Something wrong with your sandwich?" he asked, trying to make it sound light.

"No, it's okay."

"Tye," Mac reached over and as gently as he could pushed the sandwich back to the plate, "you don't have to be afraid. I won't be mad."

"Promise."

Mac fought the tightening of his muscles. "Promise," he said.

"Can I have a sandwich with your bread and peanut butter?"

Jesus! Why hadn't the kid asked him before he'd made the first one? He felt his fists clench.

No. He should've thought to ask. Christ, he'd been here almost a month, he knew all about Kathleen's granola and vegetable habits. Peanut butter without sugar in it. How stupid could you get? And brown bread. Not Mac's type of thing at all, so he'd been forced to put up a supply of real food: white bread, Kraft peanut butter, Kraft dinner, all the essentials. He'd cooked for Brad and Tye from his stash when Kathleen wasn't around and Tye had loved the forbidden food. Mac should've remembered that.

"How's about you give me your sandwich and I'll make you another one?" Mac smiled at his nephew, a little less the fishhooks this time.

"It's okay, Uncle Andy." Tye took another nibble and bravely chewed it. Mac reached over and took the sandwich out of his hands.

"It's okay, Tye. I'm not mad." And he kept telling himself that. The kid was only being a kid. Only expecting him to be a normal adult, not flying off at the littlest thing.

But the fire still smouldered in his stomach, waiting for some tinder, waiting for the slightest wind to fan it. All it'd taken with Nicole was her turning her boom box up too high.

He quickly made the second sandwich, breathing deeply as he did so. Just a kid. Just like Nicole was being that day. But they'd been trapped inside then, too. Mac looked out the window. Only five o'clock and the street lights were already on. Not that they helped. They were just small highlights in the dark wall of swirling snow. He could barely see the house across the street.

He slapped the sandwich down in front of Tye. "There you go."

"Thanks." Tye kept on looking down at the table. Mac's hand clenched as he fought the urge to reach over and yank the kid's head up. No more. Not with Tye, maybe not with anyone. Too many times in the past he'd solved problems with his fists, the way Gramps had, only to discover that he'd never really solved anything. He wasn't Gramps though. He was going to make damn sure of that. But how? The anger was still there. What could he do? Gramps had always said there were only three things to do with kids, bribe 'em, banish 'em or beat 'em. Too bad he skipped right past the first two.

Mac took a deep breath. What you'd do with a kid might be what he needed. He got up and went to the side-door closet.

"You gonna be all right for a few minutes?" he asked Tye.

"Sure." It was Tye's turn to frown. "You going somewhere, Uncle Andy?"

"Just into the garage to have a smoke." It had been his and Kathleen's compromise, and on a day like today he was damn glad she'd bent that little bit. And that Brad and Kathleen had an attached garage so he didn't have to spend even a second outside. "Finish your sandwich and play with your toys until I come back in."

"Okay." Tye took a bite out of the new sandwich and a big gulp of milk, leaving a large white moustache on his upper lip. Mac stepped into the garage and stood at the top of the steps. He zipped his parka right up to the neck. Jesus, cold enough to freeze the balls off a brass monkey, even out of the wind.

He took out his cigarettes, glad he'd rolled a bunch

in the morning. He'd learned the hard way just how tough it was to roll a smoke when your fingers were freezing. He took the first hit, felt the welcome calm in his chest, even as he shivered from the cold. The fire in his belly faded, not extinguished, but buried in a bed of ashes, safe at least for the moment.

Mac stood on the step even after the cigarette was done, thoughts of the last few years, of the fights, of Gramps, of the brawl in Maddin bar where he'd hospitalized a guy, the trial, of being released into Brad's custody all running through his head. Maybe he could change. After all, the old man was no saint, but he'd been nowhere near as quick with the belt or his fists as Gramps, and Brad hadn't come out anything like either one of them. Of course Brad had Mac and their mom to help him along the way, running interference between Brad and Gramps, Mac, the elder grandson, breaking trail, learning life's lessons the hard way. Maybe Brad could repay the favour. God knew he'd been trying the last few weeks.

Mac was so deep in thought he didn't even hear the door open behind him.

"Aren't you cold, Uncle Andy?" Tye stood at the door, shivering.

"Huh?" Mac turned and looked down at his nephew. "No, I'm not. Thinking too much I guess."

"Yeah? Mom makes me go away and think like that when I have to take a time out. Are you taking a time out, Uncle Andy?"

Mac thought about it for a second, then stepped back into the house. He ruffled the boy's hair as he went by.

"Yeah, Tye, I guess I am."

BOOGEYMEN

A ll I wanted to do was get through Ski and Terri's wedding dance without talking about my Dad. Was that too much to ask?

Apparently so.

"Ken, you're being a moron," Ski said. "You've proved your point, so why do you have to drag things out like this?"

"Like what?" I said. We were standing outside the church hall, enjoying a bit of relief from the heat and noise inside. I'd got rid of my coat and loosened my tie, but Ski had told Terri he'd keep his tux on until after midnight lunch and he was sticking to his promise.

"You know what. You wanted to show your dad you could manage without him. You did it. Now you're just rubbing his face in it."

"You act like that's a bad thing," I said.

"Don't be a dick," Ski said. He frowned. "He's got the message, Ken. Now your pigheadedness is just hurting people."

"Hurt the old man? That'd take an A-bomb."

He looked at me and shook his head. "You don't have a sniff, do you? Besides, I was thinking more about your mom."

"She's fine," I said. If I told myself that often enough, I almost believed it. "Look, Ski, this isn't the time or place for this. You've got a bunch of guests you're supposed to be visiting with."

"It's my wedding, so I can do what I want."

"Terri might have something to say about that." That was the idea. Play the trump card.

"Nice try, but Terri knows I'm out here. And why."

Shit. Ski I could handle, but having both of them rag on me was more than I needed. Still, if I couldn't use a trump, I could always cheat.

"Hey, Nolan, how's it going?" I yelled. Ski's cousin looked up from where he and a buddy were leaning on his half-ton in the parking lot. A lot cooler outside than in the hall and they could always go in when the deejay started playing more rock and roll. They'd be looking to get laid, but I figured the odds of that were between none and none. Not that that would stop them.

"Ken, man, how's it hanging?" Nolan said, lurching toward us. Definitely started celebrating early.

"Christ, Nolan, at least keep the beer out of sight," Ski said.

"No big deal," Nolan said. "There's a dance at the lake tonight. The cops will all be up there." He grinned at his own insight.

"Yeah right." Ski held out his hand. "Let's have it."

"When'd you get so tight-assed?" Nolan said. He drained the beer and handed the empty to Ski.

"Since I had to get the liquor license," Ski said. "I-"

"I think I hear Carol," I said, turning and looking into the hall. "Yep. Gotta go. See you."

Before Ski could say anything, I was up the steps, through the doors and into the hall. A pretty exit it wasn't. Actually, it was a lot closer to pathetic than pretty. Still, it got me out of a lecture and that's all that mattered.

I wondered why the whole thing between Dad and me bothered Ski so much. It wasn't like the old man and I were hurting anyone. I'd just gotten sick of being treated like a not overly bright two-year-old. Dad had never listened to any of my suggestions about how we could improve the way we did things on the farm. No, it always came down to his farm, his rules. Finally I'd had enough. I found an off-farm job I liked and used that and my own land to get by. So far it was working, and even if it wasn't easy, there was the satisfaction of standing on my own two feet, of not needing the old man. Yeah, I'd proven I didn't need him and I'd proven I didn't have to put up with his tyrannical bullshit. If he didn't like that, tough. He'd just have to learn to live with it. And it wasn't as if it wasn't his fault we weren't working together. I'd tried to meet him halfway so often I'd lost track. If he wanted to talk to me he knew where I was.

Yes. He knew where I was. If he wanted to make the effort I'd meet him halfway for the first time. Otherwise, I could wait. Of course, I expected to wait a long time. Ski may figure I was stubborn, but where did he think I got it from? It sure wasn't from Mom.

I shook my head. I'd been in a good mood before Ski brought up Dad. Hopefully I could reclaim that mood. I needed three things for that. A drink, my girlfriend, and nobody yapping at me about Dad.

Two out of three ain't bad.

While I waited at the bar, Terri's sister, Tanya, walked by. I grinned. First time I'd been to a wedding where the bridesmaid, or matron of honor, or whatever the heck Tanya was called, wasn't stuffed into some hideous excuse for a dress. No, what she was wearing was simple and cream coloured. Classy. Of course, Ski and Terri had kept things as simple as their families would let them. One person apiece standing up for them, tapes instead of a band, and the decorations in the hall to a minimum. Only thing on the walls was a banner below the portraits of the Queen and Prince Philip. Sheldon and Terri, August 21, 1993. And didn't Ski love having his hated first name hanging over his head at supper.

When I got my beer I walked over to the table where Carol was sitting with Brad and Kathleen MacAllister. I sat down and gave Carol a quick kiss on the cheek.

"You didn't talk to Ski very long," she said, raising her voice to be heard over the music.

"Everyone wants to talk to him. You know how it is." Maybe coming inside would help after all. It was hotter than hell, but talking over the music was tough. Might help keep people from ragging on me.

"Uh-huh." She looked at me for several seconds, then shook her head. "He tried to talk to you about your Dad, didn't he?"

"Christ, you promised me you wouldn't get on my case tonight."

"Too bad. I'm sick and tired of this stupidity. How tough can it be for you two to talk to each other?"

"We talk," I said.

"No, you grunt at each other or use your Mom or me as intermediaries."

"Carol…" I said. I'd told her about Dad and me. Why couldn't she understand?

"Don't," she said. "You tell me all these stories about your dad, making him out to be a cross between Adolf Hitler and Attila the Hun, but I get a different picture from meeting him, a different story from your mom and all sorts of different impressions from other people. Hell, just before you came in, Brad told me the most touching story about your dad." She looked at Brad. "Does he know what happened?"

"I don't think so," Brad said. "His dad doesn't talk much, that's true."

"So, tell him the story."

Brad looked at me. "You interested?"

"Will it keep everyone off my back for a few min-utes?"

He laughed. "For a couple, anyway."

"Go ahead then." I sipped my beer and tried to calm down.

"Not here," Brad said. He nodded toward the side door. "Let's go outside so I don't have to scream my head off."

"Whatever."

The side door opened onto the driveway that ran

beside the hall. Half a dozen people stood outside, having a smoke or just cooling off.

"So what's this big story?" I said. I pulled my tie all the way off and jammed it into my pants pocket. It was too hot and I really didn't care if Carol wanted me to stay dressed up. I wasn't like Brad. Wearing a suit wasn't natural for me.

"Not yet," Brad said. "First –"

"First you want to lecture me."

"Would it help?" Light from the open door glinted off his glasses as he looked up at me.

"Nope."

He shook his head. "You really do have a bug up your ass about this, don't you?"

"People need to mind their own business," I said.

"Like your family should have minded its own business when Gramps was beating on Mac and me?"

"That's different." Red MacAllister, Brad's grandfather, used to use a chunk of harness leather on Mac and Brad that was more like a club than a strap. And he'd use it for the slightest reason, especially when he'd been drinking.

"Really? Enough people minded their own business for years about it. But not your mom and dad."

"Dad was just doing what Mom wanted."

"Bullshit!" Brad stopped as several people turned to look at us. He took several deep breaths. "I don't know how you got such a screwed-up picture of your dad, but it's time someone set you straight."

"Someone like you."

"Yeah. Look, Ken, you've got this image of your Dad as some tyrant and that's just wrong. He's opinionated, yes, especially about the farm, and I don't think I've ever met anyone more stubborn, but his heart is generally in the right place. For some reason you've let him become this boogeyman to you, and that's the problem."

"A boogeyman? I'm thirty-two for Chrissake."

"But you're acting like a five-year-old." Brad held up his hand before I popped off again. "Look, I've been fighting with Mac about this kind of thing for almost a year. He had to deal with what happened with Gramps and he fought me kicking and screaming all the way. I don't have the time or the energy to go through the whole thing with you."

"So we're done here?" I knew I was being a dick, but talking about Dad brought out the worst in me.

"Not quite," Brad said. "I've still got a story to tell. Do you remember the day Mac finally took Gramps on and won?"

I nodded. We'd been eighteen, Mac and I. It'd been an ugly fight, but Mac had kicked the shit out of the old bastard. Brad and Mac had ended up at our place for a couple of weeks until things cooled down enough for Brad to go home.

"Well, when we left our place I had Gramps' strap with me. I wasn't ever giving him the chance to use it on me again. After we got to your place and you and Mac took off to get some beer to celebrate Mac beating Gramps, I went outside to your burning barrel. I lit the garbage in it, then threw the strap on top. I wasn't thinking straight, because by the time the garbage burned down the strap wasn't even singed. You know how thick it was?"

I nodded. Only in Red MacAllister's sick little world would it have been called a strap.

"Well, your dad came by, found me standing by the burning barrel, sobbing. He took one look, didn't say a word, just put an arm around me, grabbed the strap with his handkerchief and led me to the shop. He opened the door to the heater and started building a fire there. A big fire. I remember the sweat pouring off me even though the shop doors were open. Finally he opened the door of the heater and gave me the strap back. Flames were flying out the door and the heat was hitting me like a wall. I tossed the strap in and stepped back. I expected your dad to close the door, but he kept it open so I could watch the damn thing burn. He stood there and watched with me, an arm around me while I cried. I don't know how long it took for all of it to burn up but your dad was there for me the whole time. By the time it was done, I felt like the world had been lifted off my shoulders. Your dad never said much. He just smiled at me and said 'Better?' All I could do was nod. It wasn't a cure for all Gramps did to me, but it was a good start. Your dad understood that. He's not good with words, but he understands actions."

"Uh-huh." I didn't trust myself to speak. I hadn't known about that. I doubt even Mom did. It was the kind of thing she would've told me. I'd just assumed Brad threw the strap away.

"You've made your point," Brad said. "Why can't you let it go at that?"

"After eight months you figure I've made my point? You have a lot more faith in Dad than I do."

"Yes, I do." Brad sighed. "I'm not going to try to change your mind. I've got a couple of questions for you, though. And an observation."

"Shoot." Maybe once I got this out of the way I'd be free and clear. Could tell everybody I talked to Brad and needed to think on things for a while. It should be enough for tonight.

"Okay, question number one: was your dad as bad as Gramps?"

"Of course not." That was one thing, he'd never laid a hand on me.

"How about as bad as my dad?"

That was harder. Bill MacAllister had used a belt on the boys sometimes, but no worse than some other dads I'd heard of. His big problem was that he made sure he was away from home as much as possible, leaving Mac and Brad at Red's mercy.

"Probably the same," I said.

"Bullshit," Brad said. "Your dad was there for you the whole time you were growing up. And I doubt you ever got more than your hands slapped by him. He doesn't even compare to my dad."

"Okay, he doesn't. But your grandpa and Dad aren't fair examples. How about Ski's dad? Or Darchuk's? Or Hicks'? They're all a step up from mine."

"Their sons might argue the point," Brad said. "I'm not going to, though. Like I said, I used up all my energy on Mac. You'll have to get your head on straight by yourself."

"So, we're done?"

"Almost." Brad said. "I've still got my observation."

"Christ, Brad, do we really need this?"

"Yes, we do." Brad looked at me intently, face shadowed from the light bulb above the door. "It's a simple enough observation. Your dad was afraid."

"Yeah, right," I said. "Even if the old man was afraid of anything, he'd never let it show."

"Maybe not to you, but I know a bit about men who are driven by fear."

I opened my mouth, then stopped. Yes, that was definitely something Brad would know about.

"What was he afraid of?" I asked.

"I'll leave that up to you to figure out," Brad said. "I've been ignoring my wife long enough. Time to go in."

After Brad left I leaned against the wall of the hall. Dad afraid? There was a concept. Pissed off, yeah. Worried sometimes, sure. But afraid? He was one of the few people in Pine Valley who wouldn't back down from Red MacAllister.

So what would he be afraid of? Being made to look bad by his son? That would be more in the pissing-him-off category. And me doing well wouldn't make him feel any better. A poor crop could piss him off and worry him some, but that was a long way from fear. No, I couldn't see what he had to be afraid of. Brad was just fucking with my mind.

And doing a fine job of it.

I looked at the door to the hall. Music spilled out the door. Speeding things up a bit. Something I could dance to. That was the whole point of the evening, wasn't it? My boogeyman could wait.

My first stop was the can, to get rid of some beer. I was standing at the urinal, feeling a sense of relief when Mac stepped up to the urinal next to me.

"Fancy meeting you here," he said.

"Christ, Mac —"

"Jeez, can't a guy even say hello?"

"If that's all you're going to say," I said, glaring up at him.

"What else would I say?" He grinned easily, his freckled face relaxed, no sign of the redness that too much booze put there.

I finished and zipped up, hoping to wash my hands and get out the door before Mac was done. Then I stopped.

"Brad already talked to me," I said as I turned on the taps. "How about giving me some time to think on what he said."

Mac laughed. "Let me guess, the whole boogeyman thing?"

"Yeah." I pulled a couple of paper towels out of the dispenser. "I take it Red is your boogeyman."

"One of them, anyway." Mac stepped up to the sink. He'd cut out the middle step and just wore slacks and a dress shirt. He'd looked almost comfortable at the church. "Did Brad give you some questions to think about?"

"Just an observation."

Mac laughed again. "He definitely took too many psychology classes in university."

"Is that what it is?" I said. "I don't know about you, but I need a drink."

"No argument here."

I waved at Carol as Mac and I moved through the dancers, heading for the bar at the back of the hall. Nolan was just stumbling away from the bar, a drink in each hand.

"There's someone who's going to be hurting tomorrow," I said.

"I give him till midnight before he either passes out or pukes," Mac said.

I looked at my watch. A bit after eleven. Probably a safe bet.

"He's a big kid," I said. "He can probably soak up quite a bit." I heard Nolan laugh from across the room. "At least he's a happy drunk."

"Unlike someone else you know?"

"Uh..."

"Relax," Mac said. "I'm just messing with your head. Picked it up from Brad."

"Two Canadian," I said to Terri's uncle who was bartending. "You did want beer, didn't you?"

"Yeah," Mac said. He grinned. "You do realize you were babysitting again."

"What?"

"Making sure I'm drinking beer, not hard stuff. You figure I might get stupid."

"No, I don't." I doubt if I sounded very believable, since that was exactly what I was doing.

"Don't worry," Mac said. "Three reasons nothing's going to happen. One: this is only my third drink. Two: I don't get into fights at weddings. If you were paying attention, you would've realized that. Three: I've changed."

"So it was just at any other dances you'd get into a scrap?"

"Pretty much."

I thought about it for a few seconds. He was right. Bars, hockey games, all sorts of dances, but never a wedding. Strange I'd never noticed that before. I was usually the one pulling him out of those fights, after all. Or backing him up if things got ugly.

That was the past though. I'd had enough last year after a particularly ugly fight. I'd quit babysitting him, and now he figured he'd changed. I hoped so, but I'd believe it when I saw it.

"So you've got your shit together now?" I said. Mac and I moved off to one side, away from the bar. An older couple, probably relatives of Terri's, were getting up to leave, so Mac and I snagged their chairs. It was a bit quieter here, as far as we could get from the speakers without going outside. And I'd had pretty much all the outside I could handle.

"Not totally," Mac said, "but good enough for now."

"So you're going to tell me how to get *my* shit together?"

"Man, you had a big bowl of cranky flakes this morning, didn't you."

"You telling me that you're not going to tell me I should make up with Dad?"

"Not when you're dug in like this. You're a Brant. When you get planted, you stay planted."

"So why is everyone telling me to talk to Dad. Do they figure he's not planted anymore?"

"Most likely. Or in Ski's case, he's probably just tired

of driving out to your neck of the woods whenever you or your dad need a hand."

"I don't call him that much."

"Neither does your dad, but the trips add up. Especially when one or the other of you is just down the road and the only reason you won't call is pure bull-headedness."

"It's not like I ask him to do anything big. I just need a second set of hands sometimes."

"It's not the work that bothers Ski and you know it. It's the principle. You and your dad don't have to work together all the time, but you could at least do the simple shit together."

"Why should I? So he can call me stupid again?"

"Your dad never called you stupid in his life."

"What? How can you say that? You were there."

"Yeah, I was," Mac said. "That's why I know he never called you stupid. He'd call some of your ideas stupid, but that's a whole different ballgame."

"How do you figure that?" Christ, had Mac been paying attention? He'd been at our place so much, he had to have heard the old man putting me down.

"Because I don't have my head up my ass when it comes to your dad."

"I don't need this shit." I started to stand.

Mac caught my arm. "You ragged on me for years to deal with my problems and now you're going to run from yours? Sweet."

"I'm not running away."

"What do you call it then?"

"A strategic withdrawal."

"Those are just fancy words for running away. And running away never solves anything."

"So you're an expert now." Son of a bitch was using my own words against me.

"Just telling you what I was told." He sighed. "Tell you what, why don't I just ask you a couple of questions, then we can go back to telling stories about Ski before he got tied down."

"Okay, fine."

"Did your dad ever call anything you wanted to do stupid when you were a kid?"

"Uh..."

"I'll take that as a no," Mac said. "In fact, he was at all your hockey games, all the school stuff you did, he was just plain there. You've got nothing to bitch at there. That takes up to what, after high school? There you might have something to complain about. Next question. Did he call anything you did stupid that wasn't about the farm?"

"He must've."

"Nope. Not once that Brad or I could remember. In fact, he was still there for you even when you did something stupid like try to steal second when we were playing ball in Nipawin that time."

"That wasn't stupid. I almost made it."

"Almost? The second baseman could've had a smoke while he was waiting for you to slide." Mac shook his head. "All the shit you caught on that and all your dad said was 'Good try.'"

"You make him sound like some saint."

"No, not by a long shot. But he's just a man, Ken. Not a monster, not some boogeyman."

"So I'm supposed to go back to being to being treated like a kid?"

"No one is asking you to do that," Mac said. "Talk to him as man. Work out a way to be some sort of partners. He'll accept that now."

"Just like that. Wave your magic wand and he's changed."

"Not changed all the way, but enough. And all you need is for him to change enough so he listens."

"You've been hanging around your brother too much, the psychology stuff is rubbing off."

"Christ, I hope not." Mac grinned.

"Now I've got a question for you," I said. "Carol wants Dad and I talking because she wants a normal boyfriend, Ski is tired of doing stuff for us that we could easily do ourselves, and Brad figures we're hurting Mom. That explains why they want Dad and me to talk. Outside of thinking we're being stupid, why is it so important to you?"

"That it's stupid is a good enough reason," Mac said. "Or I could say that your dad was a better dad to me than my own was. That works too. Or I could just say that I'm going to sell my farm and I'd like to give you and your dad first crack at it."

"Selling... Mac, are you nuts?"

"Nope. Shitty little farm like mine isn't worth the effort. Not big enough, poor soil, too many rocks. No, it was just one more thing to piss me off."

"What'll you do instead?" I said, struggling to overcome my surprise.

"There'll be enough money left over after I pay off

all my debts so I can go to school. I'm going to get my GED this winter and then apply for agricultural mechanics at Kelsey."

"Mac, I don't know what to say."

"What's to say? The only reason I farmed was because I didn't know anything else. Never had enough to make a go of it the way things are now. Not enough interest either. A regular paycheque without all the headaches looks damn good right about now."

I nodded. A year or so of regular paycheques had gotten me thinking more and more about walking away from the farm. The problem was that I did have an interest in farming. Not in the crops so much as in the livestock. I thought for a minute. In many ways, Mac's farm was a lot like mine. Not much good crop land, but some decent pasture and hay meadows. If the old man and I were still working together it would make a nice fit. If, if, if. The story of my life with Dad.

"I don't know," I said finally. "I just don't know."

"No rush," Mac said. "Just talk about it with your dad. I can't see him calling it a stupid idea."

Probably not. Dad had always wanted more land. I didn't want the debt that good cropland brought with it, but Mac's place wouldn't go for that kind of money. And it was right next to our place. No dragging equipment to hell and gone. It could work.

"Let me think about this," I said. "This is kind of sudden."

"Sure." Mac smiled at me. "Was that so hard? All the bullshit done and now we can drink beer, dance and tell stories."

"That'll only work if everyone else gets off my back."

"I'll tell them your head has been officially removed from your ass."

"One question first. What the hell did Brad mean when he said Dad was afraid?"

"Damned if I know," Mac said, "but if I had to guess I'd figure he was afraid of losing the farm. Or of you losing it. Like your grandpa did."

Grandpa? I hadn't thought about that story for years, how Grandpa had lost the farm down by Regina during the dirty thirties and had to move north to Pine Valley and start over. Dad had been six when it happened. He barely remembered the prairies. Of course, Grandpa told the story enough times and talked about the old farm like it was heaven. I'd driven by it one time when I was in Regina for Agribition. Twice the land we had now, but God was it flat. Give me trees any day.

"You don't really think it's that simple, do you?"

Mac shrugged. "Damned if I know. It's all I can think of, though. You're going to have to figure out the rest on your own."

I nodded.

"Ready for another beer?" I asked.

"Sure, but I need a piss first. Why don't you grab us a couple and I'll meet you back with the others?"

"Okay."

I barely made it to the bar before I heard a yell from the direction of the bathroom.

"Motherfucker!"

Chairs crashed and I headed for the action. Fucking Mac. He'd said he'd changed.

I pushed through the crowd and stopped dead. Mac had Nolan Radinski pinned to the wall and a couple of our neighbours were holding on to Dylan King. Mac was talking to Nolan, but I couldn't hear what he was saying over the music. I could hear Nolan, though.

"That motherfucker —"

Mac said something to shut him up. I shook my head. "Motherfucker." The battle cry of every drunken brawl Mac had ever been in.

Finally Mac started muscling Nolan toward the door, talking all the while. I still couldn't hear what he was saying, but Nolan was clear enough, if not coherent. "Asshole...son of a bitch...prick."

"You need a hand?" I asked Mac as he wrestled Nolan by me.

"Nah. Everything's under control. Me and Nolan are just going outside for a talk, aren't we?"

"Bastard..."

"Have fun," I said as Mac pushed Nolan through the wide lane the crowd had left open for them. Better him than me. I had enough on my own plate.

I went back to the bar, grabbed a beer and looked around for Carol. Finally I saw her sitting with Mom and Dad on the other side of the hall.

I nodded and shrugged, and started toward them.

ACKNOWLEDGEMENTS

Writing a book is a solitary process, but many people have helped me along the way. The members of Notes from the Underground, Critical Mass, and McGinty Mondays have all given me insightful feedback, companionship, and support. My deepest thanks to them, and also to the two Daves, Carpenter and Margoshes, for the encouragement over the years since I was their student.

I also owe a debt to the Saskatchewan Artists and Writers Colonies and the Banff Centre for providing space to write this book.

I can't thank Edna Alford enough. She not only skillfully edited this book, but also guided its growth, as my mentor and teacher in a variety of settings.

Some of these stories have been previously published. "Princes in Waiting" appeared in *Grain* and in the anthology, *Stag Line: Stories by Men.* "Little Tyrants" appeared in *Grain.*

ABOUT THE AUTHOR

Larry Gasper grew up near the tree line in northern Saskatchewan, but currently lives in and works out of Saskatoon. Stories from this collection have previously appeared in the Coteau anthology *Stagline*, edited by Bonnie Burnard, and in *Grain* magazine. *Princes in Waiting* is his first book publication.